KATE

She strode up to him and stood facing him, her hands on her hips, her face determined and bold. **Beau** had watched her coming and thought she was ravishing. **She** *was* ravishing. **She** wore a pair of faded blue pants that fitted tight and her long legs were full and perfect inside. **She** wore a bulky gray sweater that revealed the good strong bulge of her breasts, and her red hair was pulled back and tied with a ribbon and her ears stuck out a little and her cheeks were red from the wind and she smiled her gay wide smile.

Untamed Heart

JULIA GREENE

BELMONT TOWER BOOKS • NEW YORK CITY

A BELMONT TOWER BOOK

Published by

Tower Publications, Inc.
Two Park Avenue
New York, N.Y. 10016

Chapter 1

Captain Samuel J. Hogarth began his day worrying about rocks. There was not a captain in the Royal Navy who did not worry about the rocks along the coastline of northern Cornwall. It was the graveyard of many a better ship than the *Royal Harp*, plying her weary trade from Dublin to Southhampton, being little fit in her old age for anything else. But now Captain Hogarth's thinking was taken up with a newer, perhaps more serious problem.

When his First Mate found him, Captain Hogarth was standing with a spyglass clamped to his eye. In trying to steady it against the roll of the ship, he stood with his whiskey-bloated belly looped over the scarred and green-painted taff-rail. The crew was gathered in an anxious knot amidships, all staring back at the white sails and gray hull of a vessel storming up under the fresh westerly breeze. Every now and then the Dutch quartermaster would sneak a look over his shoulder. He looked frightened.

The Mate asked, "Learned her nationality?" He felt weak, sickened by the thought of a sea-fight.

"Not yet, Ashton," Hogarth grunted, his voice half-lost in the hissing of the wake. "She isn't showing colors."

"Pirate?"

The Captain shook his head twice. "Isn't likely. Too far north. Besides, she looks clean. Saw a captured buccaneer down in the Bahamas once, regular floating hog pen."

"Carrying guns?"

"None that I can see."

"Reckon she might be French?"

"She foots along so fast you might be right. But I didn't hear of any trouble with French privateers before we sailed, at least not this far out of Channel waters. Did you, Mister?"

No, the Mate said, he hadn't.

The ship was coming up fast. It would be dark within the hours, but until then it was obvious that the *Royal Harp* had no choice but to stay on her course and hope for the best. She stood about as much chance of outrunning the stranger as a cart horse might of outdistancing a steeplechaser.

Now the sun was setting the mysterious brigantine was less than a quarter of a mile astern and somewhat to windward. Watching her skim over the gray-blue rollers, Hogarth felt reminiscent twinges of his first command, the *Eastern Rose*. A pretty sailor, by God! He wondered if the *Eastern Rose* might have outpaced the stranger. He reckoned, the hell with it. That had been too many years ago. He would never know.

The strange brig's master had set courses, tops, gallants and royals and had braced them right. Not a square inch of canvas but was taut, straining with wind. Hogarth trained his glass on the small knot of people behind the helmsman. The helmsman himself was a big, swarthy man, who looked Spanish. Behind him, in the place usually reserved for the Captain or the commanding Mate was a tall slim figure with red hair, hair which blew over the left shoulder and spread out in the wind like a flag.

"By God! It's a woman," Hogarth growled. "They've got a woman on board!"

The Mate took the glass from him and adjusted it. Sure enough, it was a woman. And on either side of her stood two men: one an older man whom Ashton thought must be the captain, and a younger man with a great mane of blond hair, whose face the Mate could not make out because he was holding a spyglass to his eye. "It must be the captain's lady," said Ashton, feeling uneasy with his own explanation.

Farther along he noted that though many men were crowding her deck, there was no evidence that they had triced up her gunport covers. Perhaps they were not carrying guns. On the stranger's stern, behind the red-haired woman, stood a group of men. Two of them could be seen working over the main gaff halyards.

Hogarth's big-knuckled hands tightened on the

rail as he said, "They're going to show colors!"

Christ! How fast that brig sailed! She was overtaking the schooner so easily, it seemed as if the *Royal Harp* rode at anchor.

A cry broke from the crew as a small blue package climbed towards the stranger's main gaff. When the brig forged abeam—just where her broadside would be the most effective—the man at the signal halyards gave them a hard jerk.

A resounding yell arose from amidships on the schooner. Into the breeze had sprung a Union Jack. Its red, white and blue showed bright against the cloudless evening sky.

Swearing a streak in his relief, Hogarth wiped his face with a faded bandanna. "Wish to Christ I hadn't sworn off liquor. I could do with one damned big drink!"

Despite the breeze, trickles of sweat were creeping from under the Mate's arms. Suddenly he whipped off his hat and led the crew in three loud cheers. He did not let his mind dwell on what would have happened to a lumbering unarmed merchantman like the *Royal Harp* had the stranger not turned out to be a friendly ship.

Hogarth lumbered over and began fumbling through the flag locker. When he bent on and hoisted the schooner's own Jack, there was no answering cry from the stranger's crew. The brig was already rushing ahead amid a lacy welter of spray.

"Well named, I'd say," Hogarth observed, worrying off a huge chew from a twist of tobacco.

Executed in dark red on the gray brig's stern, five words showed up sharp: *Gilded Lady,* Liverpool to Penzance.

Amid the gathering darkness, Hogarth set course behind the *Pembroke*, hoping that she would slacken her speed and that he would not lose her in the night.

Several hours later, Captain Hogarth stood at the wheel, watching stars break out by the hundreds of thousands. The moon, he knew, would be rising late. He yawned. Christ, but he was tired! So was everybody aboard. It had been a tense voyage. What with England recently declaring war again with Napoleon, everyone was on the lookout for French privateers or ships of the line. For a green officer, the new Mate seemed to be doing fine with his navigation. His calculations showed the *Royal Harp* to be sailing just about where she should be. If the new navigator had not been making errors all along the line, Hogarth figured they should pass Cape Cornwall and raise Land's End around daylight.

Hogarth bent to pick up his spyglass and search out the *Gilded Lady* ahead of them, but stopped in mid-motion. Had a faint sparkle of light shown ahead? He glanced at the compass. Southeast-by-east, by Jesus. It was right on course! He looked again and this time saw the light for sure before the *Royal Harp* lost it by nosing down the back of a long swell.

Hogarth cranned his snewy neck. Was that a ship under way, or a light on shore? Perhaps it was the *Gilded Lady*? At the end of five minutes, he saw another reddish-yellow light wink into existence.

As loud as he could, he yelled, "Land-ho!" down the companionway.

Almost immediately the First Mate came on deck carrying a couple of charts under his arm.

He flattened a chart under the binnacle light and checked the course. "That must be Penzance. Couldn't be anything else. There are no other towns along this part of the coast."

"Then we must have passed Land's End during the night. By God, we've made good time on this voyage!" Hogarth said, pleased with the old ship. "Can you make out any land yet?"

"Not yet. But I can see more lights, a whole cluster of them."

"Those would be the light's of Mount's Bay, Mister," was the Captain's confident prediction. "We always sight them first."

"You are sure those lights couldn't mean anything else?"

Hogarth studied the swinging compass card, shook his head. "Not with us sailing this course."

"Can you make out the *Gilded Lady*, sir?"

"Not for some hours past," Hogarth replied. "With her speed, she has probably already made it to port."

"Yes, I know this coast well. We can come in right close by keeping Lizard Head to our stern and Marazion to our starboard bow. There's a regular channel."

"Yes, sir. I can see it marked. I reckon we had better come in through the West Blue Channel?"

The Captain threw back her head but reflected for only a minute. "That's right. Coming in from the west you pick up those harbor lights on a nor'east-by-east course."

"Shall I relieve you, sir?"

"No, I'll hold on the harbor lights for a while. We won't go in very close till it's light."

"Aye, aye, sir, but we won't be in dangerous waters for a good while yet. North of here would be risky."

The Mate made a turn about the deck, making sure that all the men were at their stations. When he returned, Hogarth called out, "We're all right, mister. What we see is vessels laying in the harbor. If you skin your eyes you can just make our Lizard's Head off our starboard stern." With one hand he shaded the binnacle light and they both stared into the darkness.

The wind was dropping fast. They knew it because the steady rush of water under the bows came back clear and much slower. At last the Mate made out the hill, a dim, triangular mound of rising black coming boldly from the water. Then a long, low-lying island. The reddish-yellow lights shone at irregular intervals along the shore but the cluster marking the entrance to Mount's Bay was unmistakable.

Hogarth's spirits were rising with the thought that this particular voyage was almost over. He had felt that things hadn't gone right from the moment they left Dublin.

"Well, First, you hit Penzance square on the nose. Prettiest navigatin' I ever saw."

The Mate nodded and watched the lights grow brighter. Around fifteen lanterns were sending their rays over the water.

Hogarth turned his head and said, "First, I'll stay

11

at the wheel and hold her as she is. You go and tell the men to strike the foresail. Reckon we had better not go in much farther."

"We're all right, sir. We can go—"

The Mate's words were jolted out of his mouth for, without warning, the *Royal Harp* suddenly bucked like a spurred stallion and her bow shot high into the air. Her entire hull shuddered and her masts tottered. Then, as she settled back on an even keel, from below arose a dull grinding and rasping. Hogarth could hear the successive, terrifying crashes of objects falling about below. As quickly as it had begun the tumult subsided except for a sibilant hissing sound. The schooner resumed her smooth and silent progress.

"Christ!" The Mate picked himself up from the deck as Hogarth let go the brace he had grabbed. "There just can't be a reef 'way out here! We're on course and there's the lights of Mount's Bay."

Hogarth did not hear him. He was listening to that ominous hissing, rushing noise. He left the First Mate at the wheel and ran to the companionway. Air, blasting from the schooner's depths, beat in his face.

"You're a hell of a fine navigator!" he snarled at the Mate. "I'll skin you alive for this! You've punched a hole in her bottom."

Desperately, Ashton shook his head as he clutched the wheel. "Can't make it out, sir. 'Fore God, we're on the right course! I can't figure—"

"Shut up! Where's the nearest shallow water?"

"To port—should be," the Mate gasped, sawing hard on the wheel. "Can't—"

12

"Steer for it! We're going down."

The *Royal Harp* was filling rapidly. Hogarth realized it as he sprang for the axe which was kept handy against emergencies. His one idea was to hit another reef, but going as slow as possible. If the schooner didn't strike too hard, he might stand a chance of getting her off later. Lodged on a reef, she could not go down right away. He rained blows at the fore halyards until the gaff crumpled like the wing of a duck shot in mid-air. In a wild flutter of flapping canvas, the foresail tumbled down and its gaff raised a shower of water in hitting the sea.

Hogarth dashed aft, stood ready to drop the mainsail in the same brutally effective fashion, as quickly as another reef revealed itself. There seemed to be none near.

"Look! My God, *look*!" As he stared ahead, the mate's eyes became concentric rings of white. "See that?"

"See what?"

"The lights! They're going out!"

Cold to his fingertips, Hobarth watched the yellow-red lights blink out. Inside of a minute not one of the treacherous lights remained. Save for occasional, widely scattered spots of light, the whole low-lying shore line now lay in gloom.

"Wreckers—" the First Mate choked. "The real harbor must be somewhere to starboard—" He felt better. It really wasn't his fault the schooner had broken her back on that damnêd reef!

The schooner was starting to go down by the head. Soon her bowsprit was just clear of the surface, but the increased force of the swells testified to the presence of shallower water. Suddenly Hogarth heard a sullen booming of surf off to port, but by the dim starlight he couldn't see where it came from.

"There they are! To port!" Ashton spun the wheel.

"Hang on," Hogarth yelled at him and slashed through the main halyards.

When the schooner struck for a second time, her bottom made the same dull grinding noise. Long rollers lifted her, jacked her high onto a reef. The impact was not too hard, Hogarth hoped. A second big sea roared up, heaved the wreck higher, then pulled over her bulwarks. With an angry swirl the sea began cascading down the forecastle companionway like a line of enemy boarders. Now the whole foredeck was under water. Twice more the *Royal Harp* was lifted farther onto the reef then, with stern fairly high, she came to rest.

Hogarth heard himself saying, "If the wind doesn't make up, we ought to be safe for a while."

When he walked forward, he found the deck was submerged as far as the main hatch. Cold, lazy-sounding rollers eddied about the fore shrouds. They bellied out the half-submerged jibs until, one by one, they split or were carried away by the strain.

By the light of a moon beginning to rise over the rocks, Hogarth and his crew cut away and salvaged the sails. As a result, the thumping of the spars against the bulwarks lessened.

When Hogarth saw that the galley was still above water, he ordered a fire to be lit and a meal to be cooked for the men. It would still be several hours before first light.

Chapter 2

Captain Hogarth, sleeping on the poop deck, awoke in the early morning to the distinctive sound of oars. He roused Ashton sleeping a few yards away.

Pulling their way across the flattening sea were three oversized longboats. They carried no lights. The mate looked just long enough to make sure there were three and then gasped, "Wreckers! They're rowing out!"

Hogarth reached for the blunderbuss, but decided to leave it where it was. He said with a weary grin, "The devil with it. All we need is daylight."

The Mate was up and looking very uneasy. Hogarth guessed he was scared stiff that the wreckers were coming out to make sure they made a clean job of it. Survivors had an awkward way of causing trouble later.

The first light of dawn was enough to let Hogarth make out the three longboats expertly skirting a line of reefs. The foremost had six men at her oars and at least as many passengers crouched on the bottom.

Hogarth stood still, his unclubbed hair falling in a light brown mane over the shoulders of the blue woolen jersey he had donned during the night. Almost dispassionately he watched the wreckers approach. Two boats held back in the gloom while the other came pulling along in the lee of the reefs. The man at the steering oar was a burly fellow in a bright green shirt, but he was apparently not the leader. A tall, slender figure stood up and, swaying, with the roll of the long boat, shouted:

"Waaa-aant help?"

God help us, Hogarth thought, it was a woman's voice! Underneath the knit cap she wore, he caught a slimpse of tightly drawn-up red hair. The *Gilded Lady*! So he had been led onto the rocks after all!

Hogarth waited awhile before calling back, "What the hell would you think?"

Rocking in the long boat's stern, the red-haired woman called, "Take you ashore! Five pound' a head!"

From his vantage point on the stern Hogarth shouted, a rude oath.

Several of the longboat's passengers turned leathery faces and scowled. A couple of them shifted muskets to a handier position. They were a fearsome lot, wild and reckless in their variety of leather, felt and knit hats. Some of them looked like foreigners.

"You got my price!" the woman shouted. "And you got no small boat!"

"Go to hell!"

"Well, let us make it three pound' apiece. That's a good price, captain," the woman offered, as the steerer, a brutal looking Spaniard lacking his front teeth, sheered the boat away a little.

The woman, who from the distance had the appearance of a young boy, stood up on the stern locker to see as much as she could of the wreck.

"We are very sorry for you, captain," she said. "Too bad you should lose your ship this way."

Seesawing over the waves, the other boats pulled closer. Hogarth was not surprised to see the young blond man and the older, wizened man in charge of their long boats. Clearly this was the crew from the ship which had called itself the *Gilded Lady*. The crewmen in each boat for the most part wore checkered shirts, pea jackets and wide, very dirty canvas breeches. Some of them wore little gold rings in their ear lobes and at least a dozen carried brass hilted naval cutlasses. Unlike most British seamen, several of them wore beards.

The Spaniard in the green shirt nosed his boat through a bright patch of seaweed in the direction of the wreck. When she lay but ten feet off the beam, he looked up at Hogarth. There was no trifling in his manner and his gapped teeth showed in a taut grin.

"You going to do business with us?"

Hogarth affected sulkiness. "How else are we going to get ashore?"

"What can you pay?" demanded the woman. "We don't want to be hard on you, captain, or your men."

"Send your captain aboard and we'll talk it over."

The wreckers brought their longboat up under the

17

lee of the *Royal Harp* as deftly as a jolly boat. The Spaniard grabbed a dangling halyard and, light as a gull settling on on a piling, swung himself up onto the rail. There he paused, legs planted squarely apart, and looked things over.

The woman followed him on board. The other longboats were pulling alongside. The woman's eyes went over the hulk. She had the shrewd, appraising gaze of a bailiff taking inventory before he served the eviction notice.

The Spaniard's tongue crept out through gapped teeth to wet heavy lips. "From where did you clear?"

Hogarth told him, then added, "And what might your name be?"

"That is as it may be, my friend." The red-haired woman spoke up. "Suppose we talk terms? We have rowed a long way out to help you."

"That was most considerate of you, ma'am." Hogarth said.

The woman hooked thumbs in a broad leather belt. "Well, how much can you pay?" Her naturally translucent skin was browned to a mahogany color by the sun and the wind. Her companion had a parrot-like nose jutting out from beneath the brim of a battered and rusty black cocked hat.

"I might pay ten shillings a head."

"Not enough," the blond man said, jumping down on the deck. He tried to look into the main hatch, but there wasn't enough light to see much yet.

"Say fifteen shillings?"

"Maybe. How many aboard, Captain?"

"Eighteen, including myself."

"Only eighteen?" Some of the woman's jauntiness

departed. "Where's the rest?"

"Why?"

"You're sailing a bit short-handed, aren't you, Captain?"

"It's been difficult to come by seaman since the war broke out again," Hogarth explained curtly. "Suppose we come aft. I'll need help in moving one of my deckhands."

"What's the matter with him?"

"His leg was broken when we hit the reef."

"Let him stay as he is," the woman said sharply, "until we settle on our price. We'll help you then, no sooner."

Hogarth sighed. It wasn't going to be easy to deal with this woman, who seemed to be in charge. "How much?" he asked finally.

"Twenty shillings a man—and salvage."

"You want the cargo, too?" Hogarth exclaimed, not surprised, but outraged by her boldness.

"Prize of the sea," the blond youth said, throwing his head back with laughter.

Hogarth knew the laws of the sea as set down by the admiralties of different nations. And, though he had never encountered wreckers before, he had heard enough about their practices from other captains to know that the pretended help from the *Gilded Lady*, the deceiving lights and their timely arrival were all part of a plan to lead the *Royal Harp* onto the coastal rocks.

"Are we agreed?" the red-haired woman said abruptly.

"We're agreed," Hogarth gritted his teeth as he said it.

19

"Very well. We'll begin removing the cargo as soon as you pay the money and abandon the ship," the woman said, smiling at her victory.

The Spaniard went to the rail and threw his cockade in the air, shouting, "They're ours!"

The third longboat, also manned by twelve men, come bobbing alongside. As Ashton had predicted the boarders were for the most part men with a Cornish accent, the rest from various parts of the world. The second boat's helmsman, the one who had brought the blond man aboard, lacked an eye, and three fingers of his left hand.

Chapter 3

Down aft in her cabin Kate Penhallow was hot. She stood at the porthole watching the sea as they pushed along the north coast of Cornwall, past Gurnard's Head and St. Ives.

Kate stood pressed against the porthole staring out at the sea. After all those years, the dream still came back to her. Always the same dream. Never before or since her father's death had she been so sick with fear. Her father had made her go up and out on a heaving spar to help furl a sail. Despite all the years that had passed, she still heard her father's voice in the nightmare: "One hand on the spar, feet on the ropes. And *don't* look down!" The voice in the dream somehow didn't seem to belong to her father, but so some creature half-bird, half-man, a species to which she could never belong. The dream usually ended with her being carried off by a huge, angry bird.

Kate opened her mouth and lifted her head back to the sea breeze. There were tears running down her blanched, sweating face. She took a deep breath and turned and opened the door to the passageway. She went up the companionway and ran to the hatch. She flung it open and the cool wind hit her, but she did not feel it. She was aware only of her own thoughts and, distantly, of Sean's first throbbing chord on the guitar. Her half-brother began to sing a melancholy ballad that was vaguely familiar to her.

Sean O'Donnell was four years older than herself, nearly thirty now, the son of her Irish mother and some man whom Kate had never seen. After settling in Cornwall and marrying her father, Yeo Penhallow, her mother rarely spoke of her life across the Irish sea. Sean sat very still on the coil of tarred hempen line, with only his fingers moving over the guitar strings. In actuality, his lean body swayed constantly in counter motion to the pitching of the *Gilded Lady*, but so deftly did he manage his balance against the trim brigatine's devil dance with the wind that he seemed not to move at all.

He was so still that Kate, moving forward with great difficulty against the rising wind, stopped to gaze at him. Except for the tawny gold mane that whipped about his head, Sean might have been one of the Spanish or Portuguese seamen who had begun filtering into Cornwall after the first peace with Napoleon. His slim body was etched in the moonlight. He wore a black doublet, open from throat to navel, and full Spanish pantaloons. The broad expanse of Sean's chest, glistening with spume thrown up from the sea, was bronzed from long exposure to the wind and sun. About his lean belly, board-flat and ribbed and corded with muscle, he wore a broad sash of gold cloth, contrasting vividly with the soberness of his other garments.

Kate listened for a moment to his song, then walked forward, past the mast where Ol' Pendeen was winding rope. She did not speak to him. She did not want to speak to anyone.

Sean followed his song with a rollicking lyric of some unfortunate soul about to be hanged and a soft, drawn-out tribute to a faithful dog. The words did not matter and Kate did not listen to them. She sat in front of the foredeck cabin and just listened to her brother's voice, now thin and fading, now throbbing with romantic warmth, now filled with laughter, spilling into the night air and making the night seem like a magic cave.

Leaning against the cabin and steadying herself against the roll of the ship, Kate saw that the lights of Padestow were a lovely diamond glitter behind them and the beam from the lighthouse was no longer a scythe cutting through the darkness but a large single eye of fire winking ceaselessly at them across the waves. Kate's bright hair, the color of a scarlet hibiscus, blew about her face in the night wind. She was as slender as a willow sapling in her boy's trousers and shirt, and as graceful. Her hair hung loose about her shoulders, bright as a flame against her tanned face. Under slim brows her eyes were a smoky blue, almost gray, and flecks of gold flashed

23

in their icy depths. Her lips, blood-rose red, tender-soft, were moving, shaping words as she thought, but no sound came from them.

The sky was cloudless, the stars enormous clear. They were heading northeast and further to the east she recognized Alpha Centauri, a bright gold just over the starboard horizon, then near it the Great Pointers and hard by the Pointers, the Southern Cross, its lack of symmetry giving a strangely homemade quality to the heavens. Everywhere she looked, there were the stars which she had known since her girlhood. Yet she had rarely seen the stars bigger or clearer than from the deck of her darkened brig shouldering the heavy night on a heaving sea.

As the *Gilded Lady* made its way through the waves, the sails flapped loudly in the wind: alongside the water bubbled so thick and fast that it looked as if the ship might burst its planking. The flap of the sails, the creaking of the strained rigging, the deck trembling underneath her, the powerful thrust of the prow, the ease with which they glided forward, and most of all the night and the stars—all eased Kate's fear of the homecoming, the fear she always felt passing through the treacherous waters and rocks of the coast near Moontide. She felt elated by the thought of still being at sea, and suddenly very proud of being aboard the *Gilded Lady*, of owning her.

To the landward she looked at the still dark, shining water between her ship and the lights of Camelford. The riding lights of the moored ships, the lamps blazing on the quays, lay trembling deep in the water, side by side with the quick, clear stars, quivering, as if waiting like the ships for the dawn in order to cast off.

Kate remembered that as a child she had thought that her small village was called Moontide because on still nights, whether in the heat of summer or in winter frosts, the moon shone brightly on the lagoon which separated the village from the sea. It was only later, as she was growing up, that she learned that the name of the village was short for "Mohune's Tide"—from the Mohunes, a great family who were once lords of all these parts.

The Tide was the name of a small stream, on the right or west bank of which lay the village, less than half a mile from the sea. The rivulet, which was so narrow as it passed the houses Kate could remember the village boys clearing it without a pole, broadened out into salt marshes below the village, and lost itself at last in a pond of brackish water. The pond was good for nothing except sea fowl, herons, and oysters, and formed what the natives in that part of Cornwall called a "lagoon." It was called such for no better reason than that it was shut off from the open sea by a long, narrow strip of land, one portion of which thrust a towering headland into the Irish sea. It was on this headland that Carnforth Inn, which Kate's family had bequeathed to her along with the *Gilded Lady*, was situated. And it was on the treacherous rocks beneath Carnforth that Sir Rodger Mohune's ship had been wrecked, bringing to the bottom of the sea a priceless salvage which no one had been able to find, although many of the men from the village, including her father, had searched for it.

Sir Rodger was one of the Mohune's who had

died more than a century before and was buried in the vault under the village church, with others of his family. It was said in the village that Sir Rodger could not rest in his grave, but was always searching the shore line for his lost treasure. Others said, however, that sir Rodger roamed because of the great wickedness of his life. If that was the real reason, Kate mused, he must have been bad indeed, for the Mohunes who had died before and since his day were wicked enough to bear anyone company in their vault. Randolph Mohune, who had built the lighthouse which still stood on the headland, had used it to lure passing ships onto the rocks of the Cornish coast. It was he, in 1757, who had begun the wrecking and smuggling trades which still formed the basic livelihood for many of the people around Moontide.

But because of his lost salvage, it was Sir Rodger around whom the villagers spun their old tales. Men would have it than on dark winter nights Sir Rodger might be seen with an old-fashioned lantern moving about in the graveyard or searching along the storm-tossed coast. Those who professed to have seen him said he was the tallest of men, with beetling brows and a full black beard, coppery face, and such evil eyes that anyone who met their gaze must die within a year. However that may be, there were few in Moontide who would not rather walk ten miles around than go near his haunted places after dark. And once when Crazed Jones, a poor benighted body, was found there one summer morning, lying dead on the grass, it was said that he had come to his end because he had met Sir Rodger Mohune during the night.

The Preacher, Mr. Castallack, who knew more about such things than anyone else, had once told Kate that Sir Rodger had come to his evil fate because of his dealings during the Civil Wars. He would have it that Sir Rodger had served as a Colonel in the dreadful wars against King Charles the First, and had deserted the allegiance of his house and supported the rebels of Cromwell. For this deed he was made Governor of Menherion Castle, near St. Ives, and served in Parliament. He was appointed the King's jailer, but even to this trust he proved false. The King constantly carried a great diamond hidden about his person, a diamond which had once been given to him by his brother, the King of France. Sir Rodger heard of this jewel and promised that if it were given to him, he would wink at the King's escape.

Then Sir Rodger, having taken the bribe, played the traitor again. Coming with a file of soldiers at the hour appointed for the King's flight, he found His Majesty escaping through a window, had him led away to a more secure cell, and reported to Parliament that the King's escape was only prevented through Sir Rodger's watchfulness...

Kate smiled as she thought of Mr. Castallack telling his tale with pious wisdom, saying "So you see, my child, we should not be envious against the ungodly, against the man that walketh after evil counsels." It appears that suspicion fell upon Sir Rodger. He was removed from his Governorship and came back to his family estate near Moontide. There he lived in seclusion, despised by both the

Royalists and the Roundheads, until he died, about the time of the happy restoration of King Charles the Second. But even after his death he could not gain a peaceful rest, for men said that the treasure he had given to save His Majesty's life was lost at sea on a ship bearing it from London. Not daring to reclaim it, Sir Rodger had let the secret die with him, so must come out of his grave at night to try and get it again.

The Reverend Castallack would never say whether he believed this tale or not, but contented himself with pointing out that apparitions of both good and evil spirits are related in Holy Scriptures, but that the churchyard was an unlikely place for a man so evil as Sir Rodger to wander. However that might be, and though Kate for her sex was brave as a lion by day, and though the churchyard had been her favorite place to go as a child when she wanted to be alone, because there was the widest view of the sea, nothing could have taken her there by night.

As an older girl she had some reason to believe in the legend of the Mohune diamond. Having to walk to Camelford for Dr. Renard on the night her mother broke her leg, she had taken the path along the moors which overlooked the churchyard about a mile away. From there, she had most certainly seen a light moving to and fro about the church, where, she had told herself then, no honest man would be at two o'clock in the morning. But that had been in the years before she had realized the nature of her father's trade or how seldom people ever came to the inn.

There were few travellers along the lonely coastal road from Widemouth Bay to Camelford, even in the old days, and today, with the wars resumed against Napoleon, there were even fewer. Such visitors that stopped at the inn, Kate did not encourage to stay. For her, as for her father before her, the inn served another purpose than giving food and lodging to the weary travelier. Although the inn had been left jointly to Sean and her other brothers, Mark and Yeo, the *Gilded Lady* had been left to Mark and Yeo alone. As a girl, Kate had inherited nothing, but lived as a charge upon her older brothers, a charge which Mark and Yeo had seen fit to largely ignore while they dissipated what little money her father had left. It was not until after their deaths that Kate had inherited the *Gilded Lady*, and then only for want of another direct male heir.

The *Gilded Lady* was a lovely ship, lively and fast. Kate remembered how nervous she had been when she gave her first order to cast off, how the sails had filled and she had lifted her bow and moved out of the lagoon. When Kate stood in the wind, and the bloom of the spray settled on her face, she had felt something of what must have been her father's joy in his first command.

They had maneuvered at sea that day until it was dark. When they had put in, Ol' Pendeen came from below deck to the wheel, wiping his hands with a red bandana and his forehead with his sleeve. "By God, Katy," he said, "you sure can keep a body busy." She had. She must have swung the ship around, each time catching the wind expertly, at least a dozen times. She had spun the *Gilded Lady* in narrowing circles until the ship listed so much Kate had heard the dishes slide in the galley and the bell had started ringing by itself. Kate had found out that she was a sleek ship, quick to the hand, and there was little more that could be expected of her. She also found out that Sean and Ol' Pendeen were able seamen albeit Sean was a bit jumpy at the helm. But whatever the practical results of the drill might have been, when they went ashore after mooring, she saw that in the eyes of her crew, she had established herself as someone whose commands they would accept. She thought she caught a glint of respect even in Ol' Pendeen's eyes.

Kate sighed, remembering all the endless forms she had had to sign, the bland, round faces she had talked to in order to complete the transfer of ownership from her brothers' to herself. Then had come the seemingly endless delays in preparing the ship for sea duty, but at last the day came when the ship was in apple pie order. Every spot of brass had been polished to gold by Ol' Pendeen; there was not a scratch in the varnish on any of the rails. The table in the chartroom was so clean you could eat from it; the charts of the Cornish coast and the Channel ports were carefully rolled up and so neatly stacked in the rack that she was sure Ol' Pendeen had lined them up with a ruler. In the pen tray were three goose quills, sharpened to a lethal point.

Kate thought of Ol' Pendeen and smiled. He had been her father's bo'sun and, like most men who had spent their lives at sea, the old man had become a professional listener. He could read messages in the creak of the rigging and the way the wind hit the sails. Even smells were significant to him. He could tell from the smell in the air whether land was near.

Kate heard a footstep behind her and was suddenly aware of Ol' Pendeen standing stiffly by the foredeck cabin. She did not mind the old man being there. She was over the shame of her dream now, the shame she felt at the weakness of her sex, at not having been the third son her father had always wanted; now the dream was just a bad joke that she played on herself.

"Why don't you go back to your bunk and try to sleep?" Ol' Pendeen said. "The dream won't come again."

"I just want to sit here. I'll be all right."

"Sure, you'll be all right. Let's have a drink," Ol' Pendeen said, pulling a bottle of rum from his pocket.

"Why not? But I wish I could sleep."

Ol' Pendeen stirred uneasily. It was difficult to know what to say to Kate when she got into one of her moods. He sat next to her. "It won't be so bad," he said. "You'll feel different when we get past the reefs and then it won't be so bad."

"It's up here, old man." Kate tapped her head. "It's up here, Pendeen. I can still see my father lying on the deck. The flash of the pistol going off in Captain Maskelyne's hand. Then the blood. That's my problem, Pendeen. And I can't do anything about it."

"It's no good trying to live it over again. You can't change anything."

"No, you can't change anything. It's like when you see a man you remember and you still want him. But you can't have it with him anymore. Oh Jesus!"

"Forget about him, too."

"It's still up here, Pendeen," Kate said. "You spend your whole life thinking about something you did wrong. You're not going to stop your mind from thinking about it, are you? Not me anyway—Jesus, I wish I could sleep!"

Kate hesitated a moment before she took the bottle from Ol' Pendeen, twisted the cork out and took a swallow. The run tasted foul. But after the third drink, she didn't feel sorry for herself anymore. She might even have talked herself into believing that money was all there was to her ventures with the *Gilded Lady*, if she hadn't had that last drink. The rum did not make her drunk; it made her see things clearly. She was just a woman terrified out of her wits, a coward like all the rest of her sex, trying to sip courage from a bottle. That was the nasty part about it; she knew how she would feel if she gave up the inn and the *Gilded Lady*, left them both to Sean and went away, to America perhaps. It would be as if her father had died all over again. The life she led, the inn and the ship, were all that tied her to her father's memory, all that kept him still alive. But he was dead, Kate reminded herself. That was the problem. He was dead and there was nothing that could ever be done to change that.

She wondered if the sexton, Ebenezer Farrish, had finished yet with the new tombstone. He had been a good friend to her father and had kept the small wood-working shop at the bottom of the village. He was with the contrabanders when their ketch was boarded that June night by the Government schooner. People said that it was Magistrate Howard of Menherion Manor who had put the

Revenue men on the track; they said it was because after he bought the property from the last of the Mohunes, he lacked the funds to maintain it, that he turned the men in for the reward—to pay his taxes. Anyway he was on board the *Advent* when she overhauled the ketch. There was some show of fighting when the vessels first came alongside of one another, and Captain Maskelyne drew a pistol and fired it off in Yeo Penhallow's face, with only two gunwales between them. In the afternoon of Midsummer's Day, the *Advent* brought the ketch into Moontide, and there was a squad of constables to march the smugglers off across the Tamar River to Dartmoor Prison. The prisoners trudged up through the village, ironed two-with-two together, while people stood at their doors or followed them, the men greeting them with a kindly word, for they knew most of them as Bogin or Launceston men, and the women sorrowing for the wives of the men. They had left her father's body in the ketch.

Once she had the ugly scene again firmly fixed in her mind, she took the rum from Ol' Pendeen's hand. She felt so sick with fear that she sat there not even listening to the old man's rambling stories. She just had to talk with someone about her fear, dilute it by sharing it with someone else. She thought of the people with whom she could talk about it and who would make her feel better by getting frightened themselves. She could think of no one. Ol' Pendeen had already recognized her fears and braced himself against anything Kate could tell him. The only one who was impressed was Annie, the girl who sometimes served the drinks at the inn, but it was unwise to confide in people who worked for you. She wished she could tell Sean, but Sean was a man and he would just kiss away her fears and laugh at her.

"I'm glad this run is over," Ol' Pendeen said. "If we had sighted that ship-of-the-line an hour sooner, more than an hour from nightfall, we might not be here now." Ol' Pendeen paused. "I've been thinking I might just quit the trade after another few runs. It was different in the old days. You had to take your chances then, but nowadays there are too many warships on the seas, and they are faster and carry more guns than they used to. The men were different then, too. Today, you have to make your crew up from the scum of every prison from here to Africa." Ol' Pendeen spat.

"What difference does it make?" said Kate glumly.

"Well, none I guess," said Ol' Pendeen. He got up slowly and stretched. "Suppose I should be getting the Landers up and ready." Kate nodded and did not look at him.

When Ol' Pendeen had gone, Kate got up and wandered to midship and back again, a dozen times or more. The wind was coming from the west now, across St. George's channel, so that all the trees on the coastline bowed before it. There would be a storm in the morning. Now and again an old branch would tear loose from its trunk and be hurled out to sea. The waves had begun to swell, rising with deceptive, heavy slowness, as though the sea were made of thick Jamaican syrup. The brigantine ran baremasted, except for the jib and the spritsail that held her due east, so that only her narrow stern took the increasing impact of the waves. She slid down an oily gray, long trough of sea, then rose sickeningly, her bowsprit angling skyward, hanging there for long minutes before a caprice of wind and water dropped her downward again.

Standing on the deck of the *Gilded Lady*, Kate saw herself, the girl Kate, standing in the doorway of the inn with her mother, a lovely creature all pink and white and golden, whose tongue still spoke the lilting accents of Wexford. Remembering that face, a sound tore at Kate's throat—a muted syllable, voluptuous with rage, that started as an animal growl, low and bestial, and rose to a groan that was half a sob, as she remembered how the Revenue men rode through the crowds that scurried fearfully away at their approach. Kate watched the spectacle idly until a low, explosive gasp from her mother's lips reached her. She could hear her breath strangling in her throat. Then she ran, fleet as a girl, out into the crowd, and while Kate stood in the doorway as if turned to stone, she threw up her hands and caught the bridle of one of Captain John Maskelyne.

"You killed him!" she shrieked. "You killed him!"

Kate saw the man's whip go up, arching against the sky. Then it sang downward and the lash hissed across her mother's face like a serpent, cutting her cheek to the bone.

Kate saw her sitting in the roadway, holding her face in her hands, the bright blood oozing out between her fingers. Then Kate too had run, screaming, stretching out her hands to grab the man. She got a vivid impression of the man's face, swart as a Spaniard's, with a bold, jutting nose, and a chin

35

graced by a tuft of blond beard. Then one of the Protective men who accompanied the officer let down his flintlock so that the barrel came heavily across Kate's bright head. As she lay there in in the road beside her mother, with the inn reeling in circles above her, Kate heard the hoarse laughter of the Revenue men...

The vision that passed next before Kate's sightless eyes was one that she had never seen in reality, but in its curious way it was far more clear than any of the others. Kate groaned terribly, pushing her knuckles into her blue eyes and grinding them cruelly in the attempt to shut out the pictures that persisted in coming with such hideous clarity.

She could see, as though she stood there, the subterranean chamber beneath Dartmoor Prison and the brawny figure of the executioner, glistening all over with sweat, in the ruddy glow from the brazier in which the irons were heating. She could see the man's face hidden in its cap of leather that fitted over the shaven bullet head and came down to the mouth line, to form a mask through whose slits the small beady eyes shifted. In front of him, the lovely white figure of Kate's mother stretched hand and foot around the wheel that creaked as the man tightened the cords. In this fashion, the arms were dislocated at the shoulders, at the elbows, at the wrists, the legs at the hip, knee, and ankle, until at last the bones themselves gave. Then the small, willowy rods of iron stroked lightly, just hard enough to break the soft ribs of a woman's chest, until her body was a thing of rubber, lacking all skeletal support. And beside the great glistening executioner, the uniformed figure of the Revenue man asking questions in his delicate voice.

"What are the names of your husband's other companions? Where are they? Where? Where? Where?"

Kate could see her mother's fine head thrashing about on her slim throat as she moaned:

"I do not know! Truly I do not! By the Virgin! By the Blessed Infant Jesus, I do not know!"

She saw her faint. They loosened the rack and revived her. Then they began again, questioning, insisting, probing through the long hours while the irons, which had been heated for pressing against her white skin, waited. So too did the knout, the thumbscrews, the boot.

Kate stood there on the deck, swaying with the slow weaving roll and pitch of the brigantine, and her words came out hoarse-voiced: "How long did it take, my God? How long for a small and lovely woman to die?"

The sound of her voice was curiously mingled with the soft wash of the sea around the ship and with the noises inside her head.

Kate remained on deck with her thoughts until first light. When she glanced toward the wheel, it was to see the glow from Sean's pipe winking like a red star. His hands moved with the wheel but otherwise he was still, feet planted firmly, staring straight ahead. It was extraordinary the effect that so small a thing had on her, making her feel how much she was at the heart not only of the ship but also of all that was shaping ahead in the daylight to come.

She watched the morning star rise, from the

moment when it was just a flash of quicksilver on the horizon, than a pinprick of light, and finally a fiery ball.

The crew of the *Gilded Lady* began to assemble on deck. During the early years Kate had commanded her, the *Gilded Lady* had been forced to sail shorthanded, but finally the sex of her owner had been accepted, although there were still many who would not sail with a woman aboard. Now at last Kate found it possible to take her pick of seamen to man her. Of these, the greater part were English, Welsh, Irish, and Scots, but the remainder were Frenchmen from the provinces of Brittany, Normandy, and Gascony, men who had fled to the British Isles to escape punishment for crimes committed in their homeland or to evade service in Napoleon's armies.

An exception among them was Beauregard d'Auberge, or so he called himself, who had come from New Orleans. It was darkly hinted of him that he had killed several men in duels, finding that to be the simplest and cheapest way to dispose of his gambling debts. Although of French ancestry, the other Frenchmen did not like his haughty Creole manners, and were he not unquestionably the best shot among the crewmen, Kate knew that she would have trouble because of him. There were boys, too, who shipped as powder monkeys and cabin boys, and one or two runaway Negro slaves. Kate had appointed Sean her first mate, and the two of them always stood by while Ol' Pendeen and Honoré Dumas read the sailing articles to the new men, the former in English, the latter in French.

Above the mastheads the dawn sky was lightening, utterly cloudless: The wind, still freshening, sent them along at a merry clip. The mighty headland of Moontide grew out of the sea, blue, dim, and misty, discernible long before the closer-lying land at its feet could be seen.

Looking at the disappearing night, Kate sighed. It would have been far more to her advantage had it been cloudy, the stars hidden and no moon showing. It would have been better had they arrived an hour sooner when it was still dark. Once before such a dawn landing had almost cost her her life, but now there was no time for such reflections.

The barrels of wine and liquor were tied together and floated toward the shore, the longboats splashed into the sea and quickly loaded. The oarsmen sat at their benches like shadows, their gnarled hands gripping the broad sweeps. The blades of the oars had been muffled with rags. They moved out now from the lee of the brigantine, the men bending and straightening slowly, their motions stiff and hampered by their attempt to avoid all sound. Quietly the longboats crept forward, making scarcely a ripple on the sea. Kate lifted her eyes toward the fading stars. If there were Protective men waiting for them, who knew when, if ever, she would again see the stars? She lowered her head again toward where the sun was burning a track across the water. It was necessary for them to cross this, and there lay their chief danger. Here in the lingering blue shadows of the night, the longboats were all but invisible, but in the sunlight, they would stand out like targets.

Kate leaned forward. "Double beat!" she whispered.

The men bent forward, grunting with the effort,

their belly muscles knotting with the pull of the oars. Then they hauled back and the longboat shot ahead. They raced full into the sun, running over the surface of the sea. Than at last, they gained the protective shadow of the headland.

"Unload the cargo and wait until you see the light from the inn before you bring it up the cliff," Kate whispered to the boatmen. She and Sean went over the side, wading through the surf, their jackboots slung over their shoulders, their bags of powder and shot tied about their necks. As they made their way up the cliff path, the treacherous, winding path which led to the rear of the inn, they could hear only the low splashing of the men as they carried the booty ashore. Though Kate would not have admitted it to Sean, a feeling of awful loneliness had come over her.

Chapter 4

The following night, as Kate stepped out into the street, she found the wind had calmed down and the storm no longer seemed certain. It was a poor street at best, though she could remember from her childhood when it had been finer. Now, there were not two hundred souls in Moontide, and the houses that held them straggled sadly over half a mile, lying at intervals along either side of the road. Nothing was ever newly made in the village; if a house needed repair badly, it was pulled down, and so there were toothless gaps in the street, and over-run gardens with broken-down walls, and many of the houses that still stood looked as though they would not be standing much longer.

The sun had set, and it was already so dark that the lower or sea end of the street was lost from sight. There was a little fog or smoke wreath in the air, with a smell of burning weeds, and that first frosty feeling of the autumn that makes people think of glowing fires and the comforts of long winter evenings to come. Everything was still, but Kate could hear the tapping of a hammer farther down the street. There were no trades in Moontide except fishing, and Kate knew that the sound must be from Ebenezer Farrish the sexton, who was lettering her father's new tombstone. She found him in a shed which opened on the street, bent over his mallet and graver. He had been a mason before he became a fisherman, and was handy with his tools, so that if anyone wanted a headstone set up in the churchyard, he went to Ebenezer to get it done. Kate leaned over the half-door and watched him for a minute, chipping away with the graver in the bad light from a lantern.

Ebenezer looked up and, seeing her, said, "Here, Kate, will you come in and hold the lantern for me. 'Tis but a half-hour's job to get all finished."

Kate stepped in and held the lantern, watching him chink out the bits of Portland stone with his graver and blinking whenever the chips flew too near her eyes. The inscription stood there complete, but he was putting the finishing touches to a little sea piece carved at the top of the stone, which showed a schooner boarding a cutter. She read the inscription, which was not yellow with lichen as she remembered the old tombstone, but boldly and finely cut. It read:

Sacred to the Memory
of
YEO PENHALLOW
Aged 67, who was killed by a shot fired from
the schooner *Advent*, June 21st, 1805

Of life bereft (by fell design),
I mingle with my fellow clay.
On God's protection I recline
To save me on the Judgement Day.

There too must you, cruel man, appear,
Repent ere it be all too late;
Or else a dreadful sentence fear,
For God will sure revenge my fate.

The Reverend Castallack had written the verses,
and Kate had learned them by heart from a copy he
had given her. The whole village had rung with the
tale of her father's death at the time, and there were
still people who talked about it.

"Ay, 'twas a cruel, cruel thing to fire on a man so
old," Ebenezer was saying as he stepped back a pace
to study the effect of a flag that he was chiselling on
the Revenue schooner, "and trouble is likely to come
for the other poor fellows taken last week, for
Lawyer Bunting says that three of them will surely
hang at the next assize. I recollect," he went on,
"thirty years ago, when there was a bit of a scuffle
between the *Rose of the West* and the *Pembroke*,
they hanged four of the contrabanders, and my old
father caught his death of cold what with going to see

43

the poor chaps turned off at Dorchester, and standing up to his knees in the river Frome to get a sight of them, for all the countryside was there, and such a press there was no place on land . . . There, that's enough," he said, turning again to the gravestone. "On Monday I'll line the ports in black, and get a brush of red to pick out the flag. Now, Kate, I've done your work, so why do I not go up to the inn and there I'll have a word with Emlyn, who sadly needs the talk of kindly friends to cheer him, for he's getting old. And could you find it in your heart, Kate, to give me a glass of Hollands to keep out autumn chills?"

Kate threw back her red hair and laughed, having known the end to which the old man's story would come, then took him by the arm and together they wound their way up the long headland path to the inn.

As they walked silently, she felt as she had when she was a young girl wandering on the moor, with the great crag of Kilmar dwarfing the neighboring hills, until she became aware of the little path of light thrown from the inn across the ground. Now and then she could catch the sound of voices again, and then there was silence; somewhere far away on the highroad a horse galloped and wheels groaned and then the silence settled again. As they came closer, she could hear the sound of heavy things being dragged along the flags in the downstairs passage, bumping against the walls.

Five wagons were drawn up in the yard outside. Three were covered, each drawn by a pair of horses, and the remaining two were open farm carts. One of the covered wagons stood directly beneath the porch, and the horses were steaming.

Gathered round the wagons were some of the crew and the men who had been drinking in the bar earlier in the evening: the cobbler from Launceston was standing near the front window, talking to the horse dealer; the sailor from Padstow had come to his senses and was patting the head of a horse; Pete the Pedlar who had argued violently with Beau d'Auberge was climbing into one of the open carts and lifting something from the floor. And there were strangers in the yard whom Kate had not seen before. She could see their faces clearly because of the brightness of the moonlight, a brightness which seemed to worry the men, for one of them pointed upwards and shook his head, while his companion shrugged his shoulders, and another man, who had an air of authority, waved his arm impatiently, as though urging them to make haste. Then the three of them turned at once and passed back to the porch and into the inn. Meanwhile the heavy dragging sound continued. That would be, Kate thought, the goods set aside for Sean and herself, being taken down the sea-path to the village.

Kate did not know the men, but she trusted Ol' Pendeen's judgement in matters of sale. Because the horses were steaming, she knew they had come over a great distance—from the Devon coast most likely—and as soon as the wagons were loaded they would make their departure, passing out into the night as silently as they had come.

The men in the yard worked quickly, against time. The contents of one covered wagon were not taken from the inn, but were transferred to one of the open farm carts drawn up beside the drinking well across the yard. The bartering and resale of goods had already begun. The packages varied in size and description. Some were large parcels and some were small and others were long rolls wrapped in straw and paper. When the cart was filled, the driver, another stranger to Kate, climbed into the seat and drove away.

The remaining wagons were loaded one by one, or the packages were carried by the men into the darkness. All was done in silence. Those men whom Kate had seen shouting and singing earlier that night were now sober and quiet, bent on the business at hand. Even the horses seemed to understand the need for silence, for they stood motionless.

John Merlyn came out on the porch, Pete the Pedlar at his side. Neither wore coat nor hat, in spite of the cold air, and both had sleeves rolled up to the elbows.

"Is that the lot?" John called softly and the driver of the cart nodded and held up his hand. The men began to climb into the carts. Some of those who had come on foot to the inn went with them, saving themselves a mile or so on their long trek homeward. They had not left Carnforth Inn unrewarded; all carried burdens of some sort: boxes strapped over their shoulders, bundles under the arm; while the cobbler from Launceston had not only burdened his pony with bursting saddlebags but had added to his own person as well, being several sizes larger around the waist than when Kate had seen him arrive.

So the wagons and carts departed from Carnforth, creaking out of the yard, one after another in a slow procession, some turning north and some south when they came out onto the highroad, until they had all gone and there was no one left standing in the yard but the Pedlar and John, the manager of the inn.

Then they too turned and went back into the house, and the yard was empty by the time she and Farrish arrived at the inn. As they crossed the porch, she heard them go along the passage in the direction of the bar, and then their footsteps died away and a door slammed.

There was no other sound except the husky wheezing of the clock in the hall and its sudden whirring note preparatory to striking the hour. It chimed six times and then ticked on.

Chapter 5

Lulled by dancing flames and the odor of spiced
Madeira mulling on a little brass trivet, Beau
d'Auberge mused somewhat drunkenly on his
favorite seat by the taproom's chimney corner. Only
vaguely did he hear the sound of the horses
clip-clopping over the ground as the smugglers
pulled out, the distant rattle from the village of the
watchman's staff as he dragged it along a picket
fence, and the soft *slap-slap* of cards on the other
side of the room.

When Kate's voice and that of old Farrish
sounded in the passageway, Beau sat up, surprising
himself by his alertness. John Merlyn heard them
too, and hitched a leather apron more firmly around
a belly which, as he walked to the door, jiggled gently

under a red and white striped waistcoat. The whist players—Scots, Beau judged from their lack of conversation—turned their eyes, following a young black boy who had come running out of the kitchen.

Beau abstractedly watched as Kate came into the room and dabbed at her long red hair, smoothed her skirt and rearranged a set of dingy ruffles edging her bosom. He smiled faintly at the familiar routine. Katy wouldn't be a bad looking bedmate, he thought, if she'd half take care of her appearance and stop playing the man. The wench had been blessed with a luscious, big-boned figure and her regular features bore an inexplicable suggestion of good breeding. She had, moreover, a complexion which, had it not been so tanned, most of the women in New Orleans would give their best earbobs to possess. But what attracted him most to Kate was the genuine, to-hell-with-everything warmth of her smile and certain changes he saw in her very wide set blue-green eyes.

Absently, Beau speculated on when Kate might decide to replace that beer splashed blouse and her oft-spotted blue and white calico skirt. Why in God's name, he wondered, did she work so much about her own place? She had the money to have help about her. Ah, but she was a sly lass, though. When she bent to serve old Farrish his glass of Hollands and mop the lead-topped bar, he could see her biting her lips to deepen their redness.

Kate fixed him a look, maliciously wistful, appraising his worn bottle-green coat and white sailor's pants. Despite his drunkenness, Beau lounged not ungracefully across the chimney corner bench. For the thousandth time she noticed how his scarred left eyebrow, set a bit lower than his right, lent him a quizzical expression. She was sure it set other girls asighing. And the way the dark brown hair grew into a point on his forehead. For once, she noticed, his long unwashed hair was neatly clubbed at the nape of his neck with a broad swallow-tailed ribbon of lincoln green. She pondered again what kind of weapon could have given his rather thick nose that slight swerve to the right. Once more she decided it was attractive rather than disfiguring.

"Your loving Frenchie is late tonight. Have you sentenced him to heavy duty, or has that new man from Wales put his nose out of joint?"

"Not at all, Beau," replied Kate demurely and breathed vigorously upon the tumbler she was polishing. "Dumas and I still keeps company. He's a great comfort, is Dumas, and such a funny little monkey you wouldn't believe. But he *is* on watch tonight."

"So the light of your life is out on the dark waters. Fixing to marry him, Kate?"

"Oh, la, sir," said Kate mockingly, Honoré will do for a—a passing fancy, but when I tie up, I'll be wanting something better." Kate laughed and peered intently into a copper pot set among an uneven rank of vessels before her. "Some lad with a bit of quality to him "

"And it's quality you should have, my love. Such a complexion and figure would be wasted—thrown away on a hang-dog." Beau threw back his head and laughed.

A strange sort, this man, Kate reflected. A girl

couldn't ever tell what he was really thinking, or how much he meant of what he said, and he said the oddest things. The strangest thing of all about him was the way he kept his hands to himself. Sometimes Kate experienced a secret sense of grievance because of this. Maybe she wasn't good enough for a young gentleman who had once been a rake-hell about New Orleans? Maybe that was it, but every other buck in her crew, young or old, had sooner or later made an attempt to attract her. And no matter how furtive that attempt may have been, it never escaped Kate's wary eye.

Her thoughts raced on, keeping pace with her busy hands. When the day came and she had enough money to buy the Mohune house and property in Penzance and somebody who *was* somebody married her, Kate vowed she would never so much as look at another man. Never. She didn't care about looking at men, anyway—indeed, she did not. In proof of which she found herself looking at Mr. Beauregard d'Auberge. Now why would a man like him want to be lonely? But lonely he was tonight and no mistake, despite the be-damned-with-you look in his lazy, gray-blue eyes.

The dog which had been asleep under one of the tables sprang up barking as Kate's half-brother appeared on the threshold.

"Well, Katy! It was a good run we had of it last night," he called, limping the length of the taproom. The effects of an old bullet wound in his left knee joint had not yet worn away. "Hell's fire! It's fit to freeze a man's what-have-you off on the water tonight—and when I rowed in from the ship, the damned tide was against me all the way."

After greeting the whist players, he stamped over to the fire to warm his legs. "Kate! A brace of rumbullions! As fast as you can brew 'em!"

"You've had enough, Sean," Kate said with smouldering annoyance.

"Ah, be a love," Sean said laughing. He flung an arm about Kate's waist and, without effort, heaved her up to a seat on the bar. Her breathless annoyance grew louder when, after fumbling with the hems of her voluminous petticoats, Sean said, "Dammit, sister, where *is* your garter?"

"Like myself, Sean, it's become undone." Laughing, Kate pushed him away and went to fetch his brace of rumbullion. It was difficult for her to refuse Sean anything when he was in one of his moods.

The card players and a couple of mahogany-faced crewmen who had witnessed Sean's arrival with more than casual interest, turned, grinning.

The negro boy from the Barbados came shuffling in, his skin slate gray with the cold. He carried a bundle, shapeless because it was so swathed in blankets.

"You, Alcibiades, take Lucifer into the kitchen to get warm," shouted Sean.

Beau's crooked brow rose. "What have you got in there? The last remaining virgin in Cornwall?"

A low, wicked, delightful chuckle arose from Sean. "What Alcibiades carries, my man, is the one and only gamecock in this part of England who can whip the lights and livers out of Darius the Great."

"So?" At the thought of a game, Beau's face lost

52

its lonesome look. "I presume you have some money left from your share of the spoils last night?"

Sean rubbed his hands. "Aye, but I'm warning you, my American friend, Lucifer's a terrible piece of work. He killed Billy Simpson's Napoleon last week and never got scratched himself. How's your fine, brave bird?"

"Darius the Great and I stand ready to oblige, sir."

"There, Sean, I put enough Jamaica and Barbados in this to thaw you out from head to foot." Kate smiled, offering a huge, steaming rummer, bright with strips of orange and lemon peel and sprinkled with cloves and bits of cinnamon. "I warrant it'll warm your best friend, too."

"He can stand a bit of thawing," Sean agreed, black eyes a-glitter. "Well, Beau, here's a hot corner of hell for a certain Scotch factor!"

Beau noticed that one of the whist players, a small man whose face under an untidy scratch wig looked wizened and brown as a berry, burned and looked hard at Sean over his shoulder.

"Are you threatening Fergus MacThomson again?" he inquired.

"I am!" Sean jerked a gloomy nod and his shadow mimicked him on the pine paneling behind. "I am! I don't reckon that damned leech will rest a happy man until he's plucked me as clean o' me worldly goods as the Campbells plucked the MacDonalds.

John Merlyn came bustling forward, a fixed smile on his ruddy features. "Come, come, men. No bitching about like old washerwomen."

Kate leaned over the bar, her eyes showing clearly

53

that she was intent upon creating a little trouble. "Have you heard, Sean? Fergus here is betting a pound on Beau's bird."

"Let him make it two and it's done."

The nut-faced man nodded glumly. "It's done!"

"Let us hope such confidence will be rewarded." Beau laughed.

"Is your bird fit, man?" Sean queried.

"Fit as a fiddle. I keep hot bricks under his cage."

Kate, hugely delighted, bawled, "Alcibiades!" so loud that the lad came stumbling out of the kitchen with his mouth still full of duck.

"Lad, wipe your mouth and ride down to Camelford, to the Elephant and Castle, and let the folk know that Darius the Great is matched. Then to to the Harp and Crown and pass the word. If any man has a bird to match, tell him to fetch it along."

A short while later the low-ceilinged taproom reeked with tobacco smoke, wet wool, liquor fumes and pungent body smells. Already two pairs of stags, green birds never before pitted, had been matched and fought.

Hard put to fill so many mugs and tankards, Kate was sweating like a June bride, as her brother Sean put it.

Small feathers drifted about, settling on men's coats and in their hair and soon bright blood specks began to stain the sanded floor of the inn's portable cock pit. When it came time for the main bout, smoke hung in a blue nimbus about a huge ship's lantern suspended from the rafters. The atmosphere would have been worse but the door kept opening and shutting. The dog, banished to the backyard in the interests of fair play, mourned as a bitter rain began to fall.

Beau, his cuffs stripped back from forearms dark with hair, was entirely serious. Gambling always sobered him up. He used a piece of broken glass to scrape Darius the Great's spurs to a carefully calculated point. The horny growths were thin now, and keen, nearly as deadly as the steel gaffs so much favored in New Orleans.

Kate smiled and roared welcome to every man who came in. Rum and Holland gin were going faster than ale now.

Satisfied, Beau tucked his bird under one arm and called, "Sean! Reckon we're ready." The auburn bird pecked savagely at his wrist, then flicked his head, glaring defiance at the assembled men from clear, sherry-colored eyes.

The crowd gathered closer together. "Ain't that quill a living bastard?"

"Look at them spurs."

"And them eyes! Colder eyes I've never seen."

"That's a good bird, Beau. Good luck to ye."

"Who'll take two to one on Beau's quill?"

"Weights, give us weights," called some Scotsman with one eye. "I'll no' bet till we hear the weights."

Sean's bird, a wiry Dominique, weighed four pounds six ounces. He had the advantage of three ounces. This caused some shifting of the odds, but the quiet smile never left Beau's face.

"Bring it to him, Emperor," he whispered while lifting Darius the Great, restless and belligerent, off the scales. "Our war chest is getting mighty low."

The crowd had begun to shove and jostle good-naturedly for position.

Across the pit of yellow pine planks, Sean, stripped to his shirt, sweated hard while he trimmed his rangy red Dominique. Lips compressed, he was deftly shortening his bird's longest wing feathers. He was afraid that when his cock tired, his pinions might foul the enemy's spurs. Watched by his anxious backers, he then trimmed the bird's ruff. This would make it hard for red-eyed Darius to find a hold. Sean's eyes glistened now, very steady between narrowed lids. His hands trembled just a little. Kate knew that he had bet too much on the match.

Still smiling but serious, Beau elbowed his way to the pit and stepped into it. His heels made a soft grating sound on the sand. To see better, Kate hoisted herself onto the bar.

"Will you judge, cap'n?" Beau asked Kate, then hastily added, "You agreeable, Sean?"

Sean, busy biting gently at Lucifer's close-clipped comb, nodded his blond head. The red cock struggled, glaring at the glossy auburn bird between Beau's hands.

"Stand back, men! Don't crowd the birds!" Kate hoisted herself down from the bar, and used a spoon handle to divide the freshly sanded floor into halves. She waved the owners to diagonally opposite corners of the pit. Kate looked first at Sean and then at Beau. "Finish fight or best of three rounds?"

"Finish," both men said.

"Now stand back, men! Stand back! These birds can't fight if you don't give them room. Boys, bill your cocks!" Kate called and in an instant silence fell. Briefly the two bird's were held at arm's length, just close enough to permit them to peck at each other. Between his hands, Beau could feel Darius the Great's muscles tightening, the bird's whole wiry body a-quiver.

"On the line!" Kate ordered. Sinking onto their heels in their corners, both men set their birds on the floor, but still restrained them.

"One—two—three. Go!"

Beau and Sean stood up, hands flung wide apart, watching. At their feet a feathered flurry was sweeping the floor. Mouths open, the crowd leaned forward and began to shout for their favorites.

Twice, thrice, the fighting cocks leaped into the air, fanning themselves with shortened wings in an effort to maintain their balance. Meanwhile, their legs worked a series of lightening jabs driving the spurs forward. Only the trained eyes of veteran fanciers could follow the rain of blows. Almost at once, however, those in the know began to shift odds as one or the other cock got in a telling blow.

"Three to five on the rusty one. Three to five on Beau's!"

"Yer on!"

"Ten shillings even money on the Dom!"

"Done!"

The first flurry did no damage, left both cocks circling, necks outstretched, clipped ruffs flaring. Lazily, auburn and red feathers went drifting off among the damp and muddy feet of the onlookers.

Beau glanced up, caught Sean's dark eyes. "Another pound more?"

"Make it two! Lucifer is stronger."

"Done!"

Another two flurries slowed the cocks enough to make them pause and glare at each other. They held their wings half extended for better balance. A sudden shout made pewter mugs along the walls rattle. The Dom had charged and, fighting in a savage flurry, tumbled Darius the Great onto his back. In a flash the gamecock sprang on his opponent, pecking and slashing like the demon for which he was named.

Odds on Darius the Great sagged. Exasperated curses began to crackle through the air.

"Damn it all!"

"Four to three on yon red fowl!" croaked the Scot.

"Christ in damnation!"

"Done!" snapped John Merlyn, biting his lip.

At length, Darius the great, badly punished, broke loose and, shuffling, squared off again.

"Another pound more?" Beau's nostrils were pinched as he shot his question at Sean.

Kate's brother, squatting on his heels, merely jerked a nod.

In a murderous surge, Lucifer, sensing his advantage, charged in, rising into the air, his feet a buzzsaw. Instead of rising to meet him, Darius the Great ducked, passed cleanly to safety under his enemy.

No sooner had the red, disconcerted, landed off balance, than the auburn bird pounced on his back and drove a spur into the other gamecock's neck. A resounding roar billowed about the taproom. Bright scarlet blood spurting from his feathers, Lucifer floundered and made a valiant effort to stand. He ended by toppling crazily onto his side. Panting, punished by Darius the Great's relentless spurs and beak, he tried to scrabble away, but the keel of his breast only sketched a pathetic groove through the scattered sand and feathers.

Sean, bending low, set up a staccato, "*Cuck! Cuck!*" like that of a hen, in an effort to encourage his bird.

"Finish 'im! Finish 'im," screeched the auburn quill's backers.

Kate dropped to one knee. The way he was going, Darius the Great might get himself fastened into the other cock. If he did, the birds must be parted and Sean would be allowed to "handle" his bird.

Darius the Great began to worry the red cock's eyes with his beak.

"Ten tae to one on the red!" bawled the Scot, sweating at every pore. He only raised a laugh. Everyone could hear the breath rattling hollow in the red bird's throat. When Lucifer's head sank onto the sand, mugs hanging to the rafters rattled to the great yell Beau gave.

Tautly, Darius the Great was strutting, one fiery eye fixed on the pathetic snarl of pinkish red feathers. At last the red bird threw back his head, beat his wings and emitted a strident crow. The crowd bellowed, pounded one another on the back, called each other to witness.

Still smiling, Beau lifted his bird. Happily he suffered a series of vicious pecks when he began sponging off Darius the Great's cuts with a mixture of rum and water. Just before he picked up the bird, he took a small mouthful of rum and squirted a bit into the gamecock's bloodied beek.

After a hard fight, Darius the Great enjoyed his bit of grog as much as any prize fighter.

Chapter 6

That Kate Penhallow was a beautiful but admittedly erratic woman was common knowledge among the salvagers and smugglers between Penzance and Camelford, but never a soul would have suspected that she would risk an act of open piracy on the high seas. For Kate, the reading of her account books was enough to decide her; with more than half of a ship's cargo finding its way to the bottom of the ocean, and of what was left, less than a third useable, it was clear to Kate than it would be two years, even three before she had accumulated the sums that she required to buy the house and property she coveted in Penzance. So it was that she resolved upon a desperate venture, despite the violent-objections of Sean and Ol' Pendeen and the numerous defections of her crew.

So the old problem arose again. When the secret which had been closely held nevertheless got abroad, the news spread and there was scarcely a seaman who did not refuse flatly to sail aboard Kate's ship. But somehow she managed to find a crew.

These cold days which dragged on while the *Gilded Lady* was being armed and outfitted were among the dreariest of Kate's life. The dreariness of waiting, however, did not compare with the old familiar dreariness she felt on entering her cabin once again. From the very first day she had boarded the *Gilded Lady*, she had been aghast at the miniscule proportions of that dark little hutch which was the captain's cabin. A single porthole the size of a small pie was her only access to light and air. There was space for a very small sea chest beneath a corded bunk softened only by a thin straw mattress which she had aptly nicknamed "the donkey's breakfast."

She set her teeth. No. Hadn't she for all these years schemed to create a comfortable, if humdrum, existence? She'd manage.

In her gloomy little cabin, Kate sprawled half-suffocated on her bunk; but she could not deny that she was happier and more excited than she had ever been on land. While she was attempting to accustom her body to the constrictions of the cabin and the harsh texture of the male attire which she had once again donned for life at sea, she remained aware of the movements on deck.

Above her head, she could hear third Mate Honoré Dumas ordering the wives and the women of the crew ashore. Then followed a long flurry of orders, a creaking protest from the barrel winch and the rhythmic *clack-clack*! of pawls dropping into place; at last the *Gilded Lady's* anchor was being heaved.

As she rose and went to the small desk which held her papers and charts, Kate recognized her half-brother's voice ordering the setting of jibs and topsails. Water began to gurgle along the side as, almost imperceptibly at first, the *Gilded Lady's* fabric began to come alive. A wave of excitement shivered through.

It was the same excitement she always felt upon setting out to sea again, the same excitement she had felt when she first mounted the workman's gang plank and walked the length of the outfitting wharf, familiarizing herself with every detail of the overhauling. As the work progressed she had found herself increasingly pleased with the lines of the ship and especially that her hull had been painted a shining black and with the gunports which punctuated a broad, bright-yellow streak running the length of her beam.

Kate wasn't however, as pleased by the new figurehead. Ol' Pendeen had insisted upon doing the carving himself. The moment she saw it, Kate realized that it didn't depict a woman at all, but a helmeted mermaid who, with bared teeth, clutched a silvery trident and stared savagely straight ahead. However, she reckoned it looked fierce enough and she wisely made no mention of this possible slur on their captain to Ol' Pendeen; he obviously deemed this figurehead a masterpiece and intended no disrespect to her.

Kate's sextant, dividers, parallel ruler, chronometer and other navigational instruments had been ranged in well-carpentered frames or racks. The drawers in her desk were filled with a selection of the newest available charts of the channel and the coast of Cornwall.

Merging her slender, arched brows, Kate considered with sharp distaste a varicolored litter of papers piled on her little desk. God's teeth! How she loated that kind of work. Her frown faded and she sighed deeply with the realization that she was the only one on board who could do it. With the exception of Sean and Beau, she was the only one who could read and write well enough to keep the log. Upon her, too, fell the burden of accounting for the salvage, the prices it brought and what each member of her crew was paid. There had never been any need to train her in these skills for, even as a wide-eyed, gawky girl, she had studied her father's old account books at the inn, and pored over old logs until she knew very well how they should be kept.

Better still, at her father's urging, she had steeped herself in Bowditch's *Principles of Navigation* until she could plot a course and find a vessel's position better than a good many old-time mates.

Since it still was not time for her to go topside, Kate settled into the chair behind the desk and thoughtfully considered the roster of new hands which had signed aboard for this voyage.

Although not too many names were yet listed by Sean, Kate felt satisfied at having done better than expected in signing a high proportion of veteran seamen. What pleased Kate most was that these men represented several nationalities. In the interests of discipline and good order she had long since found it advisable not to ship too many hands of the same nationality. To do so would invite trouble through the possible formation of cliques strong enough to consider mutiny, a possibility she had always to consider because of the fact she was a woman. And in view of the dangerous nature of the cruise they were undertaking—well, it would pay to be particularly cautious.

A knock sounded at the door, then Luis Santiago, the *Gilded Lady*'s homely and enigmatic bo'sun entered and touched his cap's wrinkled leather visor, a courtesy uncommon aboard a smuggling vessel.

"Come in, Mister Santiago. How d'you make our recruiting?"

"Had luck, sir," he said, using the masculine form of address as did the other members of Kate's crew. "Mort Cooper, that old gunner's mate I spoke of, was willing to come aboard. Better still, he brought along a fellow, an armorer's mate, who's served a hitch with His Majesty. He'll sign on."

"Good. Have them make their mark and if they're sufficient sober, fetch 'em topdeck and I'll look 'em over."

"Aye, aye, sir." The Spaniard, whose wide and powerful shoulders contrasted oddly with short, bandy legs, started to turn away but paused, batting restless blank eyes. "Sir, where d'you want the round shot that come aboard today to be stowed? Just ain't room in that miserable little shot locker these ratted civilian carpenters built."

Kate rubbed her forehead. "Stow 'em in the cable tier for the time being."

Once the bo'sun had tramped off, Kate glanced out of the stern windows, watching a dory deep-laden with fish nets pull out from behind the wharf. In the distance Kate heard the deep-toned bell of the church strike six times, so she locked her desk and was pulling on a well-worn pea jacket when there came a tramping of feet along the deck and the sound of a familiar voice cursing.

Immediately identifying the third Mate Dumas's nasal French accent, Kate summoned him to her cabin. The mournful-appearing Frenchman came in wearing his thin, insolent smile on gaunt features framed in scraggly black whiskers.

"Are the carronades fully assembled?" asked the mistress of the *Gilded Lady*.

"Not yet, Katy, my love," said Dumas, a smile creasing his swarthy features. "Their carriages still need to be braced."

"Keep after 'em; no time to be lost if we are to be fit for action."

Kate watched Dumas' broad-shouldered frame disappear along the passageway. She waited a few minutes before following him on deck so that the bo'sun would have had time to assemble the new men in the crew. As she went topside, she heard Santiago roaring, "Line up! Line up abaft the main, you slew-footed scum!"

Hung-over and illtempered boatsteerers invaded the fo'c's'le, then reappeared driving red-eyed sluggards with liberal use of a cat o' nine tails. Anyone too sodden or surly to move smartly earned kicks to remind him he wasn't snoring off a carouse in some brothel.

Hands clenched in the pockets of her jacket, Kate waited, grim-face before the mainmast. The three Mates lined up a pace behind her. Kate, her long legs encased in canvas pants, had pulled her cap down, hoping she was looking relaxed, strong and capable enough to impress her new crew.

In a single rank to her right stood her four boatsteerers and the gunners who, because of their unique duties, had been accorded an equal rating. The remainder of the crew were drawn up in a swaying double rank which included both able and ordinary seamen. Among the latter were the "greenies," landsmen with no previous experience at sea. Generally these were farm boys or ranaway apprentices in search of adventure, or hard-featured characters: sots, absconding debtors and ex-jailbirds who were only a jump ahead of the bailiff.

Running cold, experienced eyes over these characters, Kate found them no better nor worse than average. As usual, Portugese, blacks and Britishers instinctively had collected into knots; the former Royal Navy men, surly now that the liquor had died in them, also were standing to one side, glaring contemptuously at the others.

Cupping hands, Ol' Pendeen bellowed, "Off hats! Harken to the cap'n."

On the disorderly deck descended a silence so complete that the rhythmic sound of the waves along the brig's side could easily be heard.

"Each man will be supplied his own powder and shot," Ol' Pendeen bellowed, and Dumas repeated the announcement in French. "No prey, no pay!"

The rows of men nodded grimly. They were quite

accustomed to such arrangements.

"Our good captain, Kate Penhallow, receives one thousand shillings in pay. Our master's mate—myself, lads—seven hundred. Our second and third mates, five hundred. The carpenter and shipwright, three hundred. The surgeon, two hundred and fifty, including medicines. All others one hundred, except the landsmen, who get fifty. Recompense to the wounded is as follows: six hundred shillings for the loss of a limb, three hundred for the loss of a thumb, an index finger of the right hand, or one eye."

"But matey," a man protested with a heavy Welsh accent, "I be left-handed!"

"Them as favors the use of the left gets the same as others do for the right," Ol' Pendeen ruled at once. "One hundred shillings for the loss of any other finger. Each man to select a partner or matelot to fight at his side, to nurse him when hurt or sick, and to inherit all his goods if he be killed and has no woman."

Ol' Pendeen paused for breath. "now for divvying up the loot," he continued. "After the pay and recompense to the wounded is taken out, we share in this fashion. Six portions to the cap'n. Two to the master's mate. One and three-quarters to the second and third mates; one and one-half to the shipwright; one and one-quarter to the surgeon. All others one share, except the landsmen, who get one-half share. Fair enough?"

"Fair enough," the throng of grimy men agreed.

"Then harken to the cap'n's words," Ol' Pendeen bellowed, aware that all the new men were making up their minds how it would feel to take orders from a woman.

Kate was in no great hurry to start talking. For several moments, her green-blue eyes shifted from one face to another, memorizing the faces of the new men.

She began to speak in short, sharp sentences. "I don't aim to talk much—just long enough to tell you how my ship's to be run. First: Never forget that *I* am the Lord God Almighty aboard the *Gilded Lady*. You'll obey my commands and those of the Mates *to the letter*—and run to carry 'em out. Second: I will not tolerate the least waste of water. We may be at sea a long time on this cruise."

Kate paused, her slender body yielding easily to the brig's slow rolling. "It does not please me to see so many 'greenies' among you—it means boat drills will have to start early.

Glaring, she strode along the line of new men. "Most of you look ox-dumb but, by God, you'll learn to box the compass in a week's time and to know the lines by name. You fail and you'll live on deck till you can pass muster."

She then took a short turn which brought her before the able seamen. "Now you know your duties or you'll wish you did; you're to work extra hard till the 'greenies' catch on."

Next Kate's brows pulled together and she stared hard at the boatsteerers. "I've never minded a hearty competition between boat crews and I'll reward efficient work but I will *not* tolerate any dirty work. Remember this: when we go for salvage, you are not paid to work for personal profit but to forward a successful voyage."

A puff of wind stirred red strands of hair escaping beneath her seaman's knitted cap. After taking another turn across the rolling deck, Kate halted, facing the entire company. "Next comes the matter of discipline," she shouted. "I have no intention of trying to run this vessle like a man-o'-war, but," her voice swelled, "but, by the Lord Harry, I'll be merciless towards anybody who disobeys orders, malingers or who even dreams of mutiny after we have made our strike. He will either swing from the yardarm or find his back stinging under the bite of the cat."

Kate could see the men asking themselves, Was this cruel-eyed, harsh-voiced bitch actually a woman?

She lowered her voice but it retained its edge. "It's time you learned that I am not the captain merely because I own this ship. I am the captain because I can run this ship and because there isn't a man jack of you who can. That I am a woman is something you'd better forget. You'll find small comfort in that." She glared deliberately along the disheveled ranks. "Remember this: everybody aboard is required to address me as 'Captain Penhallow.' You will obey my orders exactly as if I were a man and God help the man who shows me any disrespect. I'll have him keel-hauled faster than his mother dropped him."

For most of the red-eyed and still half-sodden crew it came as a shock to realize for the first time, that female or no, this was indeed their captain.

"God above!" growled one of the Royal Navy deserters, "Having a split-bottom aboard is bad enough, to have her cap'n is about the most chancy thing could happen!"

Kate's manner changed, became subtly intimidating. "Before watches are picked you'll be dismissed for ten minutes. Fetch on deck *all* firearms and any knife with a blade of six inches or longer." Kate paused, scowling. "I said *all* such arms; anybody tries to keep any back will learn what a lead-tipped cat can do to a man's back. Remember this," she added in a low-pitched but effective voice, "I'm not one to make empty promises."

Kate grew thoughtful upon observing a more than usual number of knives and pistols which thudded onto the deck to be marked and locked away in the arms chest lying beneath the main cabin.

Sean looked on when the crew lined up again, round-eyed and awed by the menace in his sister's expression. Even to him she seemed an overwhelming harridan—a red-haired beauty incongruously clad in canvas pants and a pea jacket.

"Since most of you bastards haven't sailed with me before and don't yet understand that what *I* say goes, I'll grant you a second chance to fetch the rest of your weapons. 'This time I won't punish any man who happens to come across a weapon he's missed, but if any weapons are discovered later, I'll make that man wish he'd never been born—by God I will!"

Scowling, the crew disappeared below. Ol' Pendeen said to Dumas, "Hope they believe her. 'Tis main bad luck christening such a voyage as this in blood."

The second summons to surrender weapons

71

brought four pistols and more than two dozen dirks, knives and daggers. Kate also found it significant that on this round none of the ex-Navy men turned in a weapon of any description and looked as innocent as could be.

Looking on, Beau was thinking hard. Only the officers, those closest to Kate, were allowed to carry weapons on board. But what about that pair of duelling pistols in the false bottom of his sea chest? What if they were discovered? He knew Kate well enough to know that he would suffer punishment.

Chapter 7

It was little before sunrise on the fifth day out when the Third Mate Honoré Dumas sighted the first sail, bearing north with the Gulf Stream off the Irish coast. Dumas banged on Kate's door to say that the sail was to the leeward, maybe two miles away, and that she had just hauled her wind to avoid their course. A merchantman, Dumas said she was, probably homeward bound from Liverpool to London.

The wind had dropped and the water was tolerably smooth for the Irish Sea, so Kate told Dumas that they must warn her to heave to with a warning shot. With that she hustled into her clothes and went on deck.

Kate gave orders to trick up a port, fire a gun,

hoist a British flag, haul up her courses, haul down her jib, take in her topgallant sails, and back her maintopsail—all done with a speed impossible for the merchantman they were pursuing.

Since it was their first chase, the men were excited and in high spirits, though they made an effort to remain calm, leaning over the bulwarks and spitting when asked a question and looking always at the sky before answering, though there was no cloud in sight and no change in the wind.

As they drew up on this first pursuit, Kate gave the order to clear for action. The muskets, except those of the sharpshooters, were ranged in a rack by the main hatchway; each man was at his post, a cutlass buckled at his waist or a dirk thrust into his belt; the two long guns were cleared of their screens, and laid out on the decks were boxes of grape, water buckets, tubes of wadding, rammers and sponges.

Their quarry was a slow brig of some three hundred tons. The closer they came, the more excited Kate became, pleased at what was about to happen. But as they closed in, they could see she was flying the Spanish flag. Bearing too few armaments to fight and too slow to run, the brig hove to at the first warning shot. All around the deck the men settled back on their heels, growling and swearing, while Kate, wishing to make no mistake, had Sean call out for permission to come aboard. Kate hoped to buy a few pipes of Spanish wine from her, so her crew might not brood over their failure so far to take a prize.

She was the *Dona Inez*, bound from London to Liverpool, thence back to Cadiz—a fine craft, coppered to the bends and clean as the inside of a mussel shell, which was not usual with Spanish ships. Kate had not seen many Spanish ships, but all those which she had seen were thickly crusted with dirt and smelled viciously of rancid oil, garlic and mold. To add to Kate's suspicions, she had two Englishmen aboard as passengers, one of whom was standing with the captain at the rail as they came up. Her cargo, as they discovered, was composed entirely of India goods: silks, guavas, opium, indigo, tea, ivory, carpets and spices, chief among these being ginger. It seemed unreasonable to Kate that a Spanish merchantman, plying her trade between Cadiz and England, should be laden with India goods, rather than the staples of the Spanish trade: sugar or coffee or cigars.

The captain was a Spaniard and held the backs of his thumbs and fingers against his chest when Sean sought to question him, flapping his fingers limply in the air and looking stupid as a goat.

"All right," Kate said to Sean, "bring down the sailing master and these two gentlemen."

They came down to the captain's cabin and joined Kate and Sean in a glass of Spanish wine.

"You gentlemen booked passage from Cadiz?" Sean asked them.

They said that was correct.

Sean walked around looking at them front and rear, up and down. Kate could see that he made the Englishmen nervous.

"You gentlemen have lived in Spain for some time?" Sean asked.

One of them, a small, round man with a face the

color of a slab of beef, looked helplessly at the other, a tall man with a protruding upper lip. He said quickly that they had been traveling.

"For business or pleasure, or both?"

"Pleasure," the tall man answered easily. The small, round man, Kate thought, relaxed gently in his chair.

"And where have you traveled?" Sean persisted, no more convinced than Kate herself that the ship was indeed all that she pretended to be.

"Oh," said the man with the protruding upper lip, waving his hand as loosely as if to indicate they had seen too many ports to name them all. "China, India, Ceylon, Madagascar, Brazil—"

Sean laughed. The glance of the hang-lip man shifted and wavered.

Kate poured him another sherry. "A pleasant voyage, I must say," Kate purred. "Do you make it often?"

"No, we've worked hard for a number of years, and we find it's time we enjoyed ourselves."

"Of course," Kate said, "and what might your business have been?"

The two men stirred uneasily. Kate's presence disturbed them as much as Sean's questions. They could make no sense of their situation. The round, red-faced man, in particular, Kate could sense, had again grown tense.

"Land," said the hang-lip man sourly. "We dealt in land."

"Land," said the red-faced little man.

"Where?"

"London, of course. Land and houses."

76

"Your families didn't accompany you on your recent voyage?"

"No; my wife is dead—ah—my children are too young to travel."

"So you left them with relatives?"

"Here!" he protested, "you've no right to be asking me these things!" His heavy lip was tight across his teeth, but when Kate looked at him without speaking and Sean laughed under his breath, he smiled again, albeit a trifle weakly.

"Of course," he said, "I left them with my sister; two sweet little girls and a little boy."

"And you learned to speak Spanish while selling land in London?"

"Why, yes; that is, no. I don't speak Spanish."

"Sure then, you would have been talking to the captain in Chinese when we came alongside, or was it Malay?"

The man glowered at Sean, and Kate threw her head back and laughed, her eyes dancing merrily.

At that moment, the door to the cabin was flung open and two men entered under guard. The First Mate was a squatty man with an inflamed, congested face despite the swarthiness of his Spanish complexion. His jaw bones were moving like the gills of a fish. Kate could see he wanted to question their authority, but felt he might be treading on delicate ground. There was after all no reason why they might not do with him as they wished.

"Are you the sailing master?" Kate inquired.

He hesitated, "I'm the Mate, senorita." Then he pointed at the red-nosed man, lean as a rail, who was looking fixedly at nothing and chewing busily.

"What's your name?" Kate asked him.

"His name's Michael," the mate said hurriedly.

"Michael McConnell," said the red-nosed man, a hint of sourness in his voice.

"Ah, by Jaysus, another mackerel-snapper," said Sean, smiling affably.

"I don't like it," Kate said, ignoring her brother's new-found camaraderie. "Let's see your papers."

"There is nothing wrong, senorita," the mate said. "You will find nothing out of the way."

"Let's see your papers."

He spoke hurriedly in Spanish to the captain, who glumly handed a sheaf of papers to Kate.

"Well," Kate said after perusing the documents, "you fly a Spanish flag, but you're bound to a British port from a British port with a cargo of India goods. You might as well be a British vessel."

The Mate's lumpy jaw moved convulsively. "Senorita, your suspicions wrong us. We are just poor men trying to make a living."

"I still think this vessel is British owned," Kate said. "You're flying a neutral flag to escape the French privateers in the Channel."

"No," the Mate protested impulsively.

"I'll keep these papers and you can make for the nearest port in Ireland."

"No," he protested again. "We're bound for Liverpool and Cadiz! We've got to have those papers."

"You wouldn't get to Cadiz if you tried all summer. I'm taking your navigator with me, so you'd better make a shorter voyage."

"You *can't!*" he shouted, his face a mottled brown

and crimson, like an overly ripe apple. "I can't find my way without McConnell."

"Yes, you can," Kate said. "All you need do is steer west. You've got to hit land if you do that. Columbus did it and so can you, if you know which way is west."

"This is a damned outrage," the red-faced Englishman said huskily.

"As for you," Kate went on, "suppose you show me some of the trinkets you picked up in China and Ceylon and Madagascar for your two sweet little girls. And for the little boy. And for the kind sister who has been caring for this lonely little family."

Both Englishmen stared at her.

"Well," Kate said at length. "I'm waiting. Let me see some of the things you bought somewhere except India. Didn't you bring any souvenirs home?"

"This is a damned outrage," the red-faced Englishman repeated thickly.

"No doubt," Kate returned, "but if we start exchanging outrages, we'll be here all night, and we must be on our way. As far as I am concerned, this an English-owned ship carrying English goods to an English port, and it's as plain as the nose on my face that the captain's no captain at all, but a cat's paw put aboard for you two to hide behind so you can slip past the French ships of the line. Now get your men together," Kate concluded, once again addressing the Mate. "You're going to help us shift the cargo from this ship to the brig."

"No," the Mate replied, "we will not!"

"I protest," said the man with the heavy lip, though it was plain he knew he was caught. "What's to become of the ship?"

"Well, it's a shame to harm this fine new English vessle, even if she does masquerade under the Spanish flag; but if you don't help us shift the cargo, I'm going to burn her."

"No, no," protested the Mate weakly. "I'll order our men to help you."

"Then take these men on deck," Kate said to the guards, "and have them work with the others—with the exception of the sailing master."

McConnell made no protest when Kate ordered him into a boat. "Accept my apologies," she said, "for taking you off this tidy little craft, but we shall return you to your own people in a few weeks."

He spat out of the porthole. Kate saw he was chewing slippery elm, a common practice among seamen when they ran out of tobacco.

When the men had gone on deck, Sean turned to his sister and asked, "What in hell do we want that man with us for? We're running a risk if we take him."

"We're running a greater risk if we don't," Kate replied. "It will take two weeks for news of our venture to reach the Admiralty from Wexford, which is where they'll probably make port. Otherwise, they would make port in Penzance about the same time we arrive home. We will need the extra time to dispose of the cargo. It is by far the richest we've ever had."

What answer Sean was going to make, he could not later remember, for at that moment the cabin door again swung open and Sean stared.

Kate also stared, quite taken back, for beyond the

open door, swaying to the uneasy motion of the ship, stood a slender girl, a girl in a green silk dress, her pretty arms bare to the elbow, and her hair, tightly braided around her head, the color of brass chafed bright by rubbing. As for her face, Sean thought, she was very nearly as beautiful as Kate, although her features were small and fine, in contrast to the large, bold ones of his sister.

Just then it seemed to Sean that turning from smuggling to the risks of piracy had been his sister's finest decision. "Well, what have we here?" he said in a whisper.

"Come in," Kate said gently. Silently the girl entered the cabin, accompanied by an older woman who closed the door behind them. The elder, a lean and formidable matron of some fifty winters, spread her arms as though to shield her charge from Sean's bold glance. Sean put out an arm and set the woman gently aside. He stood there a long moment, staring at the younger, a mere slip of a girl no more than eighteen or nineteen.

Kate watched her brother's face keenly. Now, she exulted, he will forget the tavern wenches of Camelford and Penzance. If blood flows in his veins, he will forget those whores for this delectable morsel!

Sean's dark eyes, cool and grave, studied the girl before him, then he reached out his hand and touched her shoulder, gently. She shrank back, her green eyes filled with terror; then the fear in them subsided a little.

"Have no fear, Sean said. "I will not harm you." His voice seemed oddly stiff to Kate.

The girl drew herself up proudly. "I would like to know the meaning of this!" she said. "What kind of people are you, to attack an unarmed ship? Why did you come aboard this vessel?"

Kate took a step toward her, looking down at her small face. "I ask the questions here," she said quietly. "What's your name?"

"And if I do not choose to answer?"

"Your ladyship would not be so unwise. I would regret having to use harsh measures."

The girl's green eyes flashed somber fire. "You would not dare, you slut!" she spat.

"Would I not?" Kate said softly. Then, turning to Sean, she said, "Fetch me that whip from the wall!"

Sean hesitated, searching Kate's face. But her green-blue eyes were impassive. Slowly, Sean took the weighted lash from its position and handed it to his sister. Kate slipped the loop over her wrist and played the nine-foot lash out along the floor. The girl stood there limply, her face ghost-white, staring at the length of black leather in breathless fascination.

"Your name, your ladyship," Kate said quietly.

Mutely the girl shook her head. Kate drew her hand far back, and held it there, but it was the older woman who broke.

"It is Paddock!" she screeched. "Don't hit her, you whore! You'll pay for this, just you wait! The Paddocks are a powerful family in London."

"No more powerful than your tongue, you bitch!" Kate snapped angrily, and brought down the whip so that its loaded tip cut through three of the woman's many petticoats. The old woman leaped back, shrieking.

"If she speaks again, tie her up, Sean," Kate commanded. "And gag her. I'm tired of her noise." She turned back to the girl. Putting out her hand, she lifted the girl's chin and gazed into her small oval face.

"No," Kate said, shaking her head. "I'm not going to whip you." The girl jerked her head away angrily. "What is your name?" Kate asked again. "The rest of it, I mean."

The girl glanced uneasily at Sean, as if seeking his help. For a moment she studied his bronzed face, the dark eyes and the gold hair like a great mane that hung down to his shoulders. She whispered, "It is Lydia. Lydia Paddock."

"Lydia," Kate muttered, "it fits you."

Lydia Paddock stood looking from Kate to Sean, her emerald eyes glittering, searching their lean faces. Finally, her gaze settled upon Sean.

"Sir," she said, "if you plan to act dishonorably toward me, I beg that you take my life instead I am innocent of men."

Sean looked at her surprised; Kate slowly, deliberately began to laugh. "Dishonor you?" she chuckled. "Lady, you flatter yourself."

The girl stiffened as though she had been struck, her mouth tightening into a thin line.

"Then set me ashore," she snapped. "I am bethrothed to a good and generous man, who will reward you. But if you harm me, I warn you he will find you." She turned to face Kate squarely. "By your speech, you are from Cornwall. Surely you must have heard the name of Captain John Maskelyne."

Kate stared at her. Then, slowly her head went back and she laughed. It was a hard, bitter sound, completely without mirth. Hearing it, Lydia drew back, instinctively afraid. Her eyes widened.

"You—you know him?" she stammered.

"Know him?" Kate echoed. "Yes, I know him. He caused the death of my mother and father. But I have sampled that man's kindness, as you call it, many times in the past. God save you from such a marriage!"

The girl shook her head and turned pale.

Kate stood there a long time, studying her face, before she turned away. "Very well, Lydia," she said, "have it your way." Then to Sean, "We will take her aboard our ship."

"Then you won't free us?" Lydia asked hesitantly.

"Until this moment, you were always free to continue with your ship; now everything has changed," Kate replied.

Sean opened the door to the passageway and pointed toward it. "I will see you safely aboard our ship," he said. "Once there you may lie down and rest. Are you hungry? You will find our food is good—and plentiful."

"Food?" Lydia echoed, the word shuddering up from her throat in tones that suggested nausea.

Sean stared at her blankly.

"Where will you sleep?" she asked suspiciously.

"If you are worried about your honor," Sean said, "I will sleep just outside your door, so that no one may enter during the night."

"And you—you'll not come in?"

Sean shook his head. "No," he said simply. "I shall not trouble you."

84

Lydia turned on him angrily, her green eyes firelit in their depths.

"Do you think I believe that? You're a man, for all your handsomeness, and all men are beasts!"

Sean studied her, his dark eyes sober. "I'm sorry you feel that way," he began.

"I have a right . . ."

Sean placed his hand inside his sash and came out with a pistol. "Here," he said, "take this. If any man enters your cabin—use it."

The girl looked up at him, her eyes widening. "Thank you," she whispered.

Something in her eyes alerted Sean to danger. "Not on yourself," he growled.

"No," Lydia said softly. "I shall not harm myself. No, I will live—and many a man shall suffer for this day!"

"Let her take the old woman with her, too," Kate said quietly.

Sean led the women into the alleyway and Kate listened to their footsteps receed. Kate stood there for a long while, staring after them, her brows knit and puzzled. She had not been surprised at Sean's sudden attraction to the girl; what had surprised her was the attraction, which as a woman she sensed in another woman, of the young girl toward Sean. She hoped all would go well with the plan that was forming dimly in her mind, otherwise she knew Sean would become difficult.

When Kate went on deck, she found that they had laid the brigantine alongside. The shifting of the cargo had begun and they continued to work at it all through the late afternoon and into the cold, calm night. By eight o'clock Ol' Pendeen, Sean and she figured there was close to twenty-thousand pounds worth of the best India goods under their hatches, to say nothing of the replenishings for the shop, kegs of Spanish wine and barrels of powder to replace that shot away in practice. When Kate went up on her own poop deck, she found the crew sluicing themselves with buckets of clear cool water from the Gulf stream which encompassed her brother's native land.

Sean sought her out on the poop deck and found her staring aft at the disappearing lights of the *Doña Inez*, her face grave and serene. Sean came up to her, his own bronzed face etched with forboding.

"Why, Kate," he demanded, "have you taken prisoners of no conceivable use to us—or of any value. More, they are an actual hindrance and a danger. Is it your intention to revenge ourselves on Mackelyne by molesting her?"

Kate turned to her brother, a slow smile lighting her eyes.

"Hold your long and worried tongue," she said. "Can't you understand what a stroke of luck this is? That girl in her small, dainty person represents almost as much wealth as we took off the *Doña Inez*."

"How so?" Sean growled. "You're devious, Kate. Explain yourself."

"The girl is dear to our captain Mackelyne and dear to her family in London. Dear enough to bring a ransom of several thousand pounds. Did you note the emerald on her finger—were we to dispatch it to Mackelyne with a note, might it not cause some concern in even his black heart? Followed later by one of her slender fingers... if he hesitates."

"That you would never do, Kate!" Sean gasped.

"Of course not. Alas, you know me too well," Kate sighed. "I wouldn't harm her. I even suspect, in some strange way, that we could become friends."

Sean frowned thoughtfully, peering out to sea. "The ransom plan sounds good," he said. "But how would you handle it?"

"I would keep her under guard at the inn," Kate began, "We can't keep her on the ship indefinitely."

"No, that would be sure to be noticed," Sean agreed. "But if she stays at the inn, she will lead the Revenue men back to us once we let her go."

"We will bring her to and from the inn blindfolded," Kate said. "While there she will be kept in the attic where she can see nothing."

"Under whose guard would you leave her?"

"Yours, of course, Sean."

"No, Kate, I couldn't trust myself."

"You won't do it?"

"That's right."

"But there is nobody else."

Sean's eyes narrowed thoughtfully. "No," he said, "you forgot Beau. You can trust Beau."

"All right then. He will be your relief."

"And yourself."

"What about it?"

Sean laughed good-naturedly. "We will need three shifts."

"Agreed then," Kate said. "Perhaps before we are done you can learn something about women—a lesson you sorely need."

"Yes," Sean sighed, "I'm ready to learn."

Chapter 8

Lydia Paddock sat alone in her room. She was as still as a statue, and almost as pale. But her young mind, alert and rebellious, was far from inactive. Behind her dark green eyes moved thoughts so daring that they frightened her. During the weeks she had been kept alone at the inn, except for her servant and Sean who visited her daily, she had had much time to think.

Everything had become confused in her mind. If only, she mused, she were not alone so much. If only she knew Captain Maskelyne better, she might understand his curious silence with regard to her ransom. If only her parents had left her more alone in his company in London, she might in time have become accustomed to him. She might some day even learn to care for him a little. What more could any woman want? He was a commander in His Majesty's fleet. His family owned three manors—all of which would one day be his. His holdings in Cornwall alone were far greater than those of many of the older London families. He owned major shares in the Levant and King Walloe mines between St. Just and Cape Cornwall. And his petition before the King for a family coat of arms would surely be honored. What else could any woman hope to gain from her marriage?

Lydia's face darkened perceptibly as the answer to her question came unbidden to her mind. There was one thing more, something which only her betrothed could give her—a son and heir. He alone could father the straight-limbed, fair-skinned lad she dreamed of; and she alone, in turn, could bring him the assurance that the name Maskelyne would not vanish...

Recalling Kate's words about the Captain, that he had slept with every whore in Cornwall, Lydia shuddered. Despite her youth, she had not been shocked or even surprised by Kate's words. Even back in London, she had sensed in Captain Maskelyne a cold, almost reptilian sensuality which had led her to suspect as much. Lydia shuddered again. How could she give herself unconditionally to him? She whispered to herself. His lightest touch froze her blood, and his caresses brought only fear and trembling. She had been told by her mother that if a woman's heart and mind are not opened to a man, her body will reject his seed. Perhaps she would never be able to have a son by Captain Maskelyne.

And herself? Would she also look elsewhere for fulfillment—even as far as the strong young man with the smouldering eyes and mane of tawny gold? Was she not really glad that she had not been delivered to Captain Maskelyne?

"Yes!" Lydia said aloud, with a fierce kind of joy. "Yes, I am glad, and I won't think any more about it!" She stood up suddenly and looked about her as though she were seeing the details of her room for the first time. Her eyes wandered over the great wooden beams which held up the roof of the inn, down over the carved furniture with its faded gilt and brightly colored leatherwork to the parquet floor. Great vases of Indian pottery stood in the corners covered with dust, frayed tapestries ornamented the walls, and everywhere there shone the dull gleam of silverware. Through the open arch of her attic room, Lydia could see the silver dishes glowing softly on the immense table of red lapacho wood—wood so heavy and strong, she had been told that it sank when tossed into the sea, so hard that it blunted the edge and shattered the handle of any axe. The dishes caught the flickering light of the candles that gutted and flared in silver sconces. These possessions, she knew, were too old to have come from any ship during Kate's lifetime. Perhaps, she thought, they had once belonged to some former owner of the inn, someone who had owned it in its great days. Or perhaps they had once belonged to Kate's family. Lydia wondered what sort of family Kate had come from.

Her old servant Susan entered the room as silently as a shadow and began brewing tea over a silver brazier, the ruddy fire of the charcoal casting a glow over her harsh features. Lydia looked past the woman toward the heavy swirling lines of the iron grillwork with which Sean and Beau had barred her windows. She had no way of knowing where she was—the windows of her room faced a blank stone wall.

Lydia halted her thoughts at last, aghast at their dark, unruly tumult. Captain Maskelyne never awoke such wild confusion within her. With him, she was the gentle, submissive betrothed who knew her duty and did it, repugnant though it might be. And it would be, she knew, no different after their marriage. She sighed and turned to Susan. The old woman stood there silently, the fragrant tea steaming in the cups she held in her hands. She took the tea and sat sipping it slowly, her eyes dark and brooding.

"Miss Lydia," the old woman whispered.

"Yes?" Lydia said without turning her head.

"You musn't be unhappy, my child," Susan said. "Soon the ransom will be paid and we'll be safely back home."

"That's not why I am unhappy."

"It's not!" The old woman's eyebrows arched in surprise. "Why then? You're a lovely child and have everything a young girl could wish. Why do you sigh? Why do I sometimes hear you weeping in your room?"

"Does it make you unhappy that I am sad?"

"Very."

"Why, Susan? Why are you concerned for me?"

"Because I have been very happy in your family's

employ," the old woman replied. "More so than I can ever tell you. You have never spoken harshly to me and are kind and gentle and considerate. I consider you as much my friend as my mistress. And it upsets me to see you in these moods. But why is it, Miss Lydia? You, who have so much..."

"I who have everything," Lydia whispered half to herself, "and yet have nothing."

Susan leaned close, her old eyes warm with sympathy. "There is perhaps a man?" she murmured. "A young gentleman you prefer to Captain Maskelyne?"

Lydia jerked upright, a flush of anger suffusing her cheeks.

"You are impertinent!" she flared, but her anger died as quickly as it had come. The smooth, kindly face of the old woman was soft with pity; and, too, a certain realism had begun to replace many of the proper ideas Lydia had been brought up with. This conflict had begun to pose baffling questions: In what way was she different from that big red-headed wench who held her captive? She had wealth, which could not buy her the happiness, the robust enjoyment of life which was Kate's. Kate would one day no doubt find herself in a real prison, not some attic, but would she, Lydia Paddock, ever be really free? When Kate finds love, Lydia mused, she goes to her man and loves him with all her body's passion; and it is a clean thing, a fine thing.

Gently she put out her hand and laid it on Susan's arm. "I was hasty," she said. "There is no other man in my life besides Captain Maskelyne."

Lydia sat talking with Susan until the tea was

finished, then the old woman went away. Lydia sat quietly for a moment, offering a short prayer for their safe return. But midway through the prayer the face of Sean interposed itself, and all unbidden, her thoughts began to whirl out of control. If, she thought, Captain Maskelyne broke their engagement because he considered her compromised— *Dear God, forgive me!*—then she and Sean.... But no, this was wickedness! It was evil to think this way. *I must not. I must not ...*

Lydia gazed thoughtfully as she heard footsteps moving about in the passageway. That would be Sean replacing Kate for the evening watch. Why is it, she mused, that though she did not love him, indeed she scarcely could say she even knew him, there was something about his face which moved her deeply?

His dark eyes were like those of a wounded dog, wretched and imploring. Since that night almost a week ago when he had come into her room and spent the evening talking with her, so that time almost seemed to stop, she had tried not to speak with him. She had dismissed him coldly that night, reading the naked, animal desire in his eyes, the absence of tenderness despite all the gallant phrases he had mouthed. To Lydia, that look had been inexpressibly shocking. Bred to a wealthy merchant class and raised in its pious beliefs, she instinctively believed that the demands of a husband were one of the crosses a woman had to bear. A lover, on the other hand, was a kind of cavalier servant who supplied poetry and romance—and demanded nothing in return.

Sean had demanded something. Were all men,

then, alike? She shook her head, trying in vain to clear it out of the confusing burden of thinking. Nothing in this life seemed to fit the patterns of her preconceived notions. For instance, she did not love Captain Maskelyne. Therefore his gallantries should have been utterly repugnant to her. But were they really? Truthfully, Lydia had to admit that she felt no real distaste toward the Captain's advances— indeed on more than one occasion she had responded to him with flirtations of her own. And wasn't it true that she felt a strange excitement in her response to Sean's animal directness? Was she then depraved, she asked herself?

She went to the bed and lay back against the pillows and closed her eyes. There were no answers to her questions. She had dutifully vowed to Captain Maskelyne when they parted in London that she would always love him, but at the moment certain features of his appearance escaped her. What kind of a love was it that after a few short weeks could not recall the exact shade of his eyes? Dark? Sean's eyes are also dark. Today "dark" meant nothing—what exactly *was* the shade of the Captain's eyes? It was of no importance, she told herself, but her forgetfulness rankled. What was important, her conscience told her, was the fact that one night soon, Sean would come to her door and she would send Susan to her own room.

For Lydia, the rest of the evening passed with difficulty. Sean paid her another of his nightly visits. Seated across the table from her, his glances dwelt more and more intensely on her face. And his eyes were naked with adoration. She wanted to warn

94

him, to tell him to turn aside his gaze, but she did not. But the more Susan prattled on, the more Lydia was sure that she had noticed, that she was uncomfortably aware of this wild and secret infatuation. The evening dragged on, every moment moving with seductive fingers over her tortured nerves. When at last it was over and Lydia found herself alone except for the old woman, she felt an inexplicable sadness, as though she had lost something forever, a moment which would never return.

Sitting in her nightdress, with Susan brushing out her long sun-blonde hair, Lydia was not even surprised at the shiver which ran through her body when she heard Sean's familiar tapping at the door. Susan prepared to answer the tapping.

"No," Lydia said, her voice high, breathless, filled with terror. "You may go—I won't need you tonight."

Chapter 9

As the war with Napoleon progressed, unarmed and unescorted merchantmen became scarcer, even in the Irish Sea. Smuggling goods from France and Spain became almost impossible because it meant running the English blockade of the French coast and the ever-present danger of French privateers. Nevertheless, Kate was resolved upon a second venture, this time against the sea traffic between Dublin and Liverpool.

However, a few days after preparations for the voyage had begun, the wind which had been blowing from the southwest began about four in the afternoon to rise in sudden strong gusts. All through the morning, they knew bad weather was due. The lights were put out on the shore in the hope that some stray vessel might be led aground. That stretch of Cornish shore had proved a death-trap to many an up-Channel sailor in a south-westerly gale. For with the wind blowing from the south, when they could not double the headland, they were almost always stranded on the shore. Kate could remember many good ships which had failed to round the headland and had beat their way up and down the coast all day, only to find themselves beached when darkness fell.

Once on the rocks, there was little need for Kate's men to attack them. The sea had little mercy. The water was deep to the shore and the waves fell over the rocks with a weight no ship timbers could withstand. Those who did try to save themselves were usually caught in a deadly undertow which sucked them off their legs and carried them out again under the thundering waves. It was that back-suck against the rocks that you could hear for miles inland, even as far as Camelford, on still nights long after the winds had sunk.

But on this night there was no wreck, only such a wind as Kate had never known before. She doubted whether anyone in the village had gone to bed. At the inn itself, there was such a breaking of tile and glass, such a banging of doors and rattling of shutters, that it was impossible for any of them to sleep. She had gone down in the middle of the night with Sean to inspect the chimneys, fearing they might collapse. The wind was at its fiercest about five in the morning. It was then that someone had run up from the village to say that the sea was breaking over the beach and that the village was likely to be flooded.

With the tides already riding high from heavy rains and the sea breaking clear over the great outer beach—a thing which had not happened for fifty years—there was so much water in the lagoon that it passed its bounds and flooded all the sea meadows.

When day broke, the lower end of the village was flooded as was the churchyard, although it stood on rising ground. Despite the damage, however, the storm was a nine hours' wonder, for the wind fell very suddenly. The water began to recede. The sun shone bright and, before noon, people came out to their doors to see the floods and to talk about the storm. Most of them said there had never been a wind so fierce, but some of the older people spoke of one in the second year of Queen Anne, and would have it that it was at least as bad, or worse.

The following day was a Sunday, and with preparations on the *Gilded Lady* Beau found himself with little to do except go down to the cabin on the beach, where he hid his rum from the rest of the crew, and see what damage had been done to his supply. He was crossing the swampy meadows strewn with shrew-mice and moles when he saw them. There was Kate on her way to church, dressed in what he supposed she thought was her finery and followed by Ol' Pendeen.

Although Beau had had the Bible and church-going habits instilled in him at an early age by his father, he was not a religious man. It was not that he was irreligious, but simply that he had once been more religious than he was then. He did not suppose that Kate had ever the slightest interest in religion. For a moment he was torn between the thought of sitting quietly on the beach with a bottle of rum and the imagined spectacle of Kate Penhallow sitting primly in a pew among all the proper people of the village. He decided he could drink rum at any hour and set off after them.

Few enough village folk came to the church at any time and fewer still came that morning. The meadows between the village and the churchyard were wet and muddy from the water. There were streamers of seaweed tangled about the tombstones. Outside the churchyard wall was a great bank of seaweed, from which came the salty rancid smell that is always in the air after a south-westerly gale had strewn the shore with wrack.

Inside the church, there were green patches down the white walls where the rain had got in and perhaps half a dozen people and as many more children whose parents had sent them regardless of the weather. The people stared at Kate as she came in, for no one had ever known her to go to church before. Some in the village said she was a Catholic, and others, an infidel. Beau decided that she had come as a favor to the parson who had written the verses for her father's headstone. She took no notice of anyone, nor exchanged greetings with those that came in, as the other people wre doing, but kept her eyes fixed on a prayer book which she held in her hand. Beau noticed, however, that she could not be following the service. She never turned a page of the book.

The church was so damp from the floods that a fire had been lit in the brazier which stood in the back. Thre was a wet cold coming up from the flagstones, and Beau sat as near the brazier as he could get. He had thought there would be more people and that Kate's presence would create more of a stir. Disappointed, he sat back, prepared to be bored and wishing he had opted instead for a bottle of rum on the beach.

The service, however, had scarcely begun when he became aware of a strange noise under the church. The first time it came was just as the Reverend Castallack was finishing "Dearly Beloved..." and he heard it again before the second lesson. It was not a loud noise, but sounded like that which boats make jostling against one another, only there was something deeper and more hollow about it. The people looked at each other. They all knew that the sound could only come form the Mohune vault under the church. Beau had heard it said in the village that it underlay half the chancel and that there were more than a dozen Mohunes buried there. It had not been opened for more than forty years, since Reginald Mohune, who burst a blood vessel drinking at the Dublin races, was buried. He had also heard the tale that one Sunday afternoon, some forty years back, such an unearthly cry had come from the vault that the parson and the people got up and fled from the Church, and would not worship there for weeks afterwards. Beau did not himself believe any of these village tales, but still he had to admit to a slight crawling of his flesh.

He had sensed a moment of panic in the congregation, but the people thought better of it and did not budge. He saw old Mrs. Parr give such starts when she heard the sounds that twice her spectacles fell off her nose into her lap. Ebenezer Farrish seemed to be trying to mask one noise by making another himself, whether by shuffling his feet or by thumping down his prayer book. But the thing which most surprised Beau was that Kate, whom he knew cared neither for God nor the Devil, looked uneasy and gave a quick glance at Ol' Pendeen every time the sound came.

They all sat quite still until Mr. Castallack was well into his sermon. Then came a noise from below louder than those before, hollow and grating like the cry of an old man in pain. Old Mrs. Parr jumped up, calling out in a loud voice to the minister, "O master, how can ye bide there preaching when the Moons be rising from their graves?" Then she ran out of the church.

That was too much for the others; they all fled. One of them was shouting, "Lordsakes, we'll all be throttled like that poor idiot boy!"

Within a minute, there was no one left in the church except Rev. Castallack, Kate, Ol' Pendeen, and Beau. Kate was clearly strong enough to give an accounting of herself even to a Mohune. The minister went on with his sermon, pretending that he neither heard any noise nor saw the people leave the church. When he had finished, Kate and Ol' Pendeen went up to him to congratulate him on his sermon, and then walked sedately out.

Beau had never felt comfortable enough in a church to wait and shake hands with the minister, so he waited for them outside. During their walk back to the inn, he asked them what they thought had caused the strange noises from the Mohune vault.

Kate had merely looked at him blankly and shrugged.

"Well, that I can't tell you," returned Ol' Pendeen, "not wishing to waste thought on such idle matters. But I will tell you this. If the floods have so damaged those walls that they need underpinning, there'll be work for old man Farrish and myself. And no bloody money in it either." He added in a whispered afterthought, "It's for the church, you know."

So the three of them came back to the inn together; but looking up at Kate once while Ol' Pendeen was making these pretences, Beau saw her eyes twinkle under her slender brows, as if she was amused at the old man's discomfort.

What thoughts are brewing in that woman's mind? Beau wondered.

Kate took out the tinder-box and candle and walked down the passage, holding the candle as far in front of her as possible. About twenty feet beyond she came upon the wall they had broken through to make a ragged doorway into the vault behind. She stood for a moment on the doorsill until the light had time to penetrate the gloom.

It was a large room, but scarcely more than nine feet in height, with the ceiling blackened by the many torches which had been lit there. The floor was of soft wet sand. The walls and roof were of stone and at one end was a staircase closed by a great flat stone—the same stone with a ring in it which provided entrance from the church above. All round the sides were stone shelves, with divisions between them like great bookshelves; but instead of books there stood the coffins of the Mohunes. In the middle of the room were stacked scores of casks, kegs, and runlets, from a storage cask that might hold thirty gallons down to a beaker that held only one. They were all marked with white paint on the end, with figures and letters that set forth the quality of each.

As Kate walked round the stack of casks, inspecting them for any damage, her foot struck one which was nearly empty, producing the same sound which she had heard earlier that day in church. It was the casks, not the coffins, which had produced that booming sound by knocking against one another.

It was plain enough that the whole place had been under water; the floor was still muddy, and the green and sweating walls showed the floor-mark within two feet of the roof. There was a wisp or two of fine seaweed that had somehow got in, and a small crab scuttled across one corner. The coffins appeared to be only a little disturbed. They lay on the shelves in rows, one above the other, twenty-three in all; most were of lead, and so could never float, but the wooden ones were turned slantways in their niches. One had floated away and been left on the floor upside down in a corner when the waters had receded.

She wondered which was the coffin of Sir Rodger Mohune and whether anything of value, rings, bracelets and such, might have been buried with them. The lead coffins had no names on them, and on such wooden coffins as bore plates, she found the writing to be in Latin and so rusted over that she could make nothing of it.

Kate had long since wanted to go through each coffin for valuables, but she had no man to help her with the lifting. Even Sean had been scandalized by the thought of robbing the dead. As though the dead would have minded! Still, it was a solemn thing to be closeted with so many dead men, knowing that all flesh would one day come to this. It moved her, too, to see pieces of banners and funeral shields, and even shreds of wreaths that loving hands had put there a century before, now all ruined and rotten—some still clinging, water-sodden, to the coffins, and some trampled in the sandy floor.

Kate spent some time searching among the coffins before her eyes were attracted to a great wooden coffin that lay by itself on the top shelf, a full six feet from the ground. Intuition told her almost at once that this was the coffin of Sir Rodger Mohune. Mounting a nearly empty keg of madeira, she inspected it with her candle. Although the coffin seemed sound enough on first glance, she found that it was wormed through and through, and that it was little better than a rotten shell, with only a thin planking separating her from the dead man. She struck the planking with her fist and her hand went clean through it in a cloud of dust and rotted splinters.

She reached inside until her fingers touched something light and wet which she supposed was a wisp of seaweed. But in the candlelight she saw that it was black and wirey. For a moment, she could not make out what she had gotten hold of; then she saw that it was a man's beard. Seeing Sir Rodger's name on a boldly lettered brass plate on the side, Kate determined to get down to the distasteful work of searching the coffin.

It would not be the first time that she had looked on death. Indeed, she had long since become accustomed to such sights, having as a little girl seen corpses washed up from the wrecks, and besides that having helped the village doctor sponge down some poor bodies that had died in their beds during an epidemic.

Sir Rodger must have been a tall man, for the coffin was of unusual length, and when she had pulled away the rotted side, Kate could see the whole outline of the skeleton which lay inside. The form itself was wrapped in the remains a woolen or flannel shroud, so that the bones themselves were not visible. The man who lay there must have been well over six feet, Kate thought. The flannel had sunk in over the belly; the end of the breast-bone, the hips, knees, and toes were easy to make out. The head was swathed in linen bands that had been white, but were now stained and discolored with the dampness. The beard had once escaped beneath the chin-band. In her blind rummaging, Kate had torn away the chin-band and let the lower jaw drop on the breast, but little else was disturbed. There was Sir Rodger Mohune, resting as he had been laid out a century before. Kate lifted the lid and reached over to see if there was anything hidden on the other side of the body.

She found nothing but one small trinket which Kate's eye told her would bring no great price. It was a locket which lay on the breast of the silent and swathed figure, attached to the neck by a thin chain which passed inside the linen bandages. A whiter portion of the flannel showed how far the beard had extended, but the locket and chain were quite black, by which Kate judged they were made of silver. The shape of the locket was not unlike a crown piece, but about three times as thick. Finding the hasp on the chain, Kate drew it out from its rotted linen folds. She had expected more, much more, and wondered if it would pay her to open the other coffins.

Scarcely was the locket in Kate's hand before she had it undone, finding a thumb-nick whereby, after a little pressure, the back, though rusted, could be opened on a hinge. She had expected little more than a portrait of one of his wives or mother, so that her curiosity was piqued when she found nothing at all except a little piece of folded paper.

Kate felt like a man who had gambled away all his property and stakes his last crown—heavy-hearted, yet hoping against hope that his luck may turn and that with this last piece he may win back all his money. Foolish though she felt herself to be, she nevertheless hoped that this paper might have written on it the exact sighting of the ship that went down containing the Mohune diamond. It was a wild hope and quickly dashed. When she had smoothed the creases and spread out the piece of paper in the candlelight, there was nothing but a few verses from the Psalms of David. The paper was yellow and showed a lattice of folds where it had been pressed into the locket. The handwriting, though small was clear and neat, and there was no mistaking a word of what had been set down.

The days of our age are threescore years and ten; And though men be so strong that they come To fourscore years, yet is there strength then But labor and sorrow, so soon passeth it Away, and we are gone.

Psalm XC; 21

And as for me, my feet are almost gone; My treadings are well-night slipped.

Psalm lXXIII; 6

But let not the waterflood drown me; neither let The deep swallow me up.

Psalm LXIX; 11

So, going through the vale of misery, I shall Use it for a well, till the pools are filled With water.

Psalm LXXXIV; 14

For thou hast made the North and the South. Tabor and Hermon shall rejoice in thy name.

Psalm LXXXIX; 6

So there it was! For all her hopes that there would be at least a ring of some value to repay her efforts, she had nothing to show for it but a few pious words. She remembered Mr. Castallack saying that Sir Rodger, after his wicked life, had desired to make a good end, and sent for a parson to console him. Kate guessed that these goodly sentiments had been hung around his neck to ease his entry into Heaven.

Before she left, Kate picked up the beard from the floor and put it in its place on the dead man's chest. She also tried to fit pieces of the coffin back in place, but that proved too difficult. She decided to leave things as they were; when the men delivered the next supply of contraband, they would think that the wood had fallen to pieces because of natural decay. It would not do to have them think she had robbed a grave; sailors were a superstitious lot.

The locket, however, she kept. She hung it around her neck under the man's shirt she wore. It was a curious thing in itself and would probably bring a small price in Penzance.

The candle had burnt so low that Kate was obliged to place a stick in it so that she could carry it without scorching her fingers. When she came to the end of the passageway, the stars and moonlight gleamed through the crevice above her head and she snuffed the candle out. Standing on a small keg, she hoisted herself up until her waist was above ground, and the was able to twist herself into a sitting position on the wet churchyard grass.

Brushing off her trousered legs, Kate rested for a moment on the flat top of a raised stone tomb which in her girlhood had been her favorite seat. There had been few girls in the village of her own age, and none whom she cared to make her companion, so that she spent long afternoon hours musing alone in the churchyard and gazing out to sea. Now, beneath her dangling legs, she saw that the crack in the ground from which she had climbed had widened still further with the recent storm. Just where the crevice came up to the tomb, the dry earth had shrunk and settled so that the hole was now a foot or more across. It would soon be time, Kate mused, for them to find a new storage place for their loot. For the moment, however, it would be enough to tell Sean that their goods were undamaged by the floods and the rains.

Kate remembered that Reverend Castallack had called her resting place an "altar tomb," and in its day it must have been a fine monument, being carved around with festoons of fruit and flowers. But it had suffered so much from the weather that Kate had never been able to read the lettering on it or find out who had been buried there. As a girl she had chosen this as "her place," not only because it had a flat and convenient top, but because it was screened from the wind by a thick clump of yew trees. These yews had once, she remembered, completely surrounded it, but on the seaward side had either died or been cut down. On the other three sides the yews grew thick and close, embowering the tomb like the high back of a fireside chair. She remembered many autumns when she had seen the stone slab crimson with fallen, waxy berries and come to collect them for her father.

Now she gazed out at the silhouette of her brig which lay at anchor on the opposite side of the lagoon. She could see men moving over her deck who were more like shadows then the men themselves. How strange it seemed to be sitting there, watching her men at their nightly tasks. She wondered if Beau might be among them. It was strange how that man kept intruding into her thoughts. What precisely was the emotion that she had begun to feel toward him? Was it love? She threw back her head and laughed at the thought. No, but it was not quite lust either. He had qualities which she had not encountered in a man before; he was a gentleman, not merely a gentleman of the contraband. Originally, Kate had disliked him because of his airs, but that had changed to a bantering between them, underneath which a more serious emotion was developing. How could she have ever disliked him for being that which she wanted most in her life?

She was, she was beginning to realize, driven by fierce surges of emotion that often ran quite counter to one another, for apart from the fact that she both liked and disliked Beau at the same time, and hated Captain Mackelyne with undying hatred, yet another current surged within her, no less strong than the others: a powerful, mounting tide of ambition. Her girlhood had been shadowed by the remembrance of what the Revenue men had done to her parents. In humble circumstances, always she had had a hunger for greatness. Wealth? She had that now. No, it was more than wealth she desired. It was a name that people would reckon with, holdings spread out from horizon to horizon, a great manor house, and tall sons to carry on the family.

Would Beau be the man to sire such sons? Kate could easily imagine him sporting the dress and manners of a country gentleman. That thought again? Angrily, she put it from her mind, and turned to planning the details of her manor, picturing it lovingly in her mind, furnishing it room by room with all the luxuries she had ever seen or heard of. The furniture would be hand-carved and brightly gilded, and on the back of each chair would be carved her crest. That thought brought her up short. Her crest! What heraldic device could she employ? What escutcheon had she upon which to charge her nonexistent armorial bearings? No, she would have to find a man who already possessed the right to such a crest.

Kate sat for an hour or more, trying to imagine what her man would be like, scheming how she would meet him once she had her great manor in Penzance.

Chapter 10

Beau decided not to caulk the longboat right away—it still looked good for another month—and he slipped over the side of the *Gilded Lady*, eased himself into the lagoon, and floated for a moment before swimming to shore. He swam toward the stretch of marshy beach near the old shack. When he reached the shore, he saw Ol' Pendeen waving to him from the ship. He waved back and flung himself down on the sand. He was thinking that if it had not been for the old man offering to take his watch, he would still be confined to the ship. Ol' Pendeen was a good man and preferred to be aboard the *Gilded Lady* than anywhere else.

Beau sat up and hunched his tired shoulders

forward. It was hot and there was no wind. He looked around at the scrawny, twisted trees, the lagoon, the sky, and the distant blue range of hills. He could never decide whether Cornwall was more beautiful during the short weeks of summer, or during those long, lingering months of autumn. In its strange wild way, Cornwall was beautiful at any time of the year, and he knew that he was content with the moment and that he would still have the memory of the contentment even after the moment had passed.

But if the distant country was beautiful, the inlet was not. Kate's people had chosen it because of its size and the narrowness of its two entrances. The shore was gray, a marshy stretch of beach. Scrub weeds dotted the lumpy sand with dark green and the debris of the ocean tide was spread along the shore; an ancient strand of rope, frayed and gray and gleaming wet; chunks of sun-bleached wood and empty rum bottles, and a faded red scarf. The scarf brought back his drifting thoughts, and he wondered about the girl who had worn it and how it had gotten there.

Beau's shack was wood and iron and scraps, a regular bird's nest of a place. Weather-worn boards mingled with discarded rum bottles and rusted metal parts. The door had been salvaged from some ship wrecked at sea, and the doorframe wasn't true and the door sat at a crazy angle, held closed with a nail and a loop of string. Since Beau had decided to use the place to store some of his booty from the trade, he had constructed a better locking arrangement. A wooden latch with a metal bolt locked it from the outside. But a strong man wanting entry could have by-passed the door anyway, and simply kicked in the walls. Beau supposed that before he had begun to use the place that it was used by the children from the town. Beau used it primarily to hide his small cache of rum. The crew would have finished off his entire stock in one night's drinking bout.

Beau struggled with the lock, disengaged it, and stumbled into the darkness within the shack. Light arrowed through chinks and cracks, touching the bare sand floor and the rumpled mattress and the scarred and battered sea chest. An unlit candle stuck into its own wax stood on top of the sea chest. It didn't fall off when Beau opened the chest to rummage through the damp clothing for his buried treasure. He brought a bottle up and went back to the door to open it.

The sunlight burned his eyes. After the third swig, he knew he wasn't going to have another drink. It happened from time to time that he reached a point, a sudden moment of surfacing, of clarity and awareness. He saw himself as others did not bother to see him.

Beauregard d'Auberge, aged thirty-five, a bright young man gone dim. He saw the bland face and the hairy body of the stranger in bed with his wife and the flat dull voice saying over and over, "It's all right, I can explain. It's all right, I can explain. Just be calm, in the name of Christ. It's all right, I can explain," and Jeanne screaming at him. And all the voices of the lost girls were one, and all were Jeanne, and Jeanne was gone. She had left him right after he had killed the man. In his fury, he had not challenged the man to a duel, but had simply shot him. And in New Orleans, they had called it murder. He had not waited for the trial, but had taken the first ship he could find bound for foreign ports.

He ducked his head away from the harsh sunlight, glittering bright on all the ugly places of the world, and decided he would have another drink, and his fingers scratched at the cork in the bottle. He knew what to do when the world crept in like that, when past and present became real and dreams were only dreams. But he must hurry or he would see himself, and he could not stand that and he did not want to have to kill himself. Anything was better than just to stop and be no more.

In his haste, the bottle slid through his fingers and fell with a soft sound into the sand. In stooping for it, he looked up and saw a woman walking toward him.

He stopped, frozen, terrified. He thought it was Jeanne, and he didn't want her to see him, to know what he had become. But then he saw it wasn't Jeanne. It wasn't any of the lost girls. It was Kate Penhallow. He quickly scuffed sand over the bottle so she would not see it. He did not want that. So now he hid the bottle in the sand, scuffling his bare feet over it, and he blinked at the girl striding down the beach toward him. He waited, lounging in his gray pants and blue and white French naval shirt beside the gray shack, hoping she would pass by so he could open the bottle and have one more drink before he went back to the shop. Behind her, he could see that wild black mare she always rode and whose name he could never remember. He thought the chances of her going by were not very good.

115

She did not go by. She strode up to him and stood facing him, her hands on her hips, her face determined and bold. Beau had watched her coming and thought she was ravishing. She *was* ravishing. She wore a pair of faded blue pants that fitted tight and her long legs were full and perfect inside. She wore a bulky gray sweater that revealed the good strong bulge of her breasts, and her red hair was pulled back and tied with a ribbon and her ears stuck out a little and her cheeks were red from the wind and she smiled her gay wide smile. She came threading her way through the sand toward where Beau was.

"Ahoy there," she said.

"Ahoy yourself," Beau said.

Kate glanced back over her shoulder, across the lagoon, shielding her eyes from the sun, to where the *Gilded Lady* lay at anchor. "I thought you were on watch now."

"Ol' Pendeen took my watch for me, so I could take a short swim."

Kate sniffed. "What are you drinking?" she asked him and made a face. Then she stooped and brushed quick fingers through the sand and brought out the hidden bottle. "Good God!" she said, more to herself than to Beau.

He was getting annoyed. Who did this damn woman think she was, to come down here where she had no business to be, to talk to him in that superior voice and make comments about his drinking? "I'm sorry," he said, trying rustily for sarcasm. "I can't afford the madeira you drink."

Kate laughed, surprising him. "I didn't think you

116

cared for wine," she said. She leaned forward staring into his face. "How old are you, Mr. d'Auberge?"

"I don't know," he said, wishing she would go away.

"You look a hundred and eighty. But you aren't, are you? You've just been looking at life the wrong way. How old? Thirty? Forty?"

Beau did not answer. He hoped that the insolence of his silence would offend his captain and she would respond with a sharp reprimand. He could then insult her with his surly, obsequious good manners. Perhaps she would then leave.

But she did not leave. "You live here?" she asked him, motioning towards the shack with a sly smile playing about her lips.

"It's my home away from home," he said.

"It reminds you of New Orleans?"

"Yes!"

"Build it yourself?"

Beau said nothing.

"Can I see inside?"

"Why?"

"Because I want to."

He shook his head, confused. "Why should I let you inside my house?" He recognized that his tongue was growing thick and thought it must be the swim that had tired him.

"Because it isn't your house and if you don't, I'll throw this bottle out in the lagoon."

"I thought you would've had me cat-whipped instead," said Beau smiling.

"No, I wouldn't do that."

"Why not?"

"You would enjoy the punishment."

Beau stared at her face and the smile dancing on it, gay and confident and arrogant, and at the bottle held loosely in her hand, and he stepped aside from the doorway to let her pass.

Inside, she blinked in the darkness and looked at the mattress and the sea chest and candle. "Light the candle," Kate said.

He started to tell her to go to hell, but she stared him with such self-assurance that he fumbled in the sea-chest for matches. When he struck the match, he saw the sand ingrained in the walls and the frayed edges around the mattress. He lit the candle and Kate bent over the mattress, rummaging among the sheets and balnkets.

"No bugs," she said and turned to look at him again. "What about you, d'Auberge? Have you got any bugs?"

"No," he said angrily, but he knew it was weak anger because she had affected him. He felt ineffectual against the hard assurance of a woman who owned a ship and commanded him. "I live on the sea," he said, trying to regain his balance. "I swim a lot."

"And you drink a lot. And you don't drown?"

"No. Not yet."

Kate patted the mattress, a soft sound in the tiny shack. "You're afraid," she said casually.

"Ma'am, you're inside, you've seen there's nothing to see," Beau said. "So give me the bottle back, right now."

"Of course. Want me to open it?"

"I can do it."

"No, let me." Kate sat down on the edge of the mattress, and twisted the cork loose with long, strong fingers. She opened the bottle, sniffed at the top, and held it to her lips. She drank long and hard, and when she handed the bottle to Beau, her eyes were red and watering. She gasped and lay back, laughing.

Beau found himself smiling in return. Her assurance grated on him, but he understood that she wanted to be friends and that she did not know how to be friends except by forcing herself on him. But he did not understand why she wanted to have anything to do with him in the first place.

As he drank, she leaned back further on the bed, resting her back against the wall. Then she held up her left hand for the bottle back. There were no rings on her fingers.

He studied Kate's face carefully for a moment, until he was sure she was aware of it. "I'll tell you, Kate, m'love, you look like one hell of a girl to be sleeping alone in that fine inn and running a crew of jacks like these. Have you ever been married, by any chance?"

She seemed startled by his words and then glanced quickly down at her left hand. "By no chance whatever, I have not. "What about you?"

Beau shook his head. "I was."

"She left you."

Beau settled his weight carefully on the corner of the opened sea-chest, careful not to over-balance it. "Yes—in a way," he said.

"You're really not one of us, are you?" Kate was giving him a long, hard look, trying to read his

119

thoughts, certain there was more to this man than there was to the others who plied their trade aboard the *Gilded Lady*.

Beau threw up his hands, almost tipping the sea chest over. "You found me in the sea," he said with restrained anger. "I am alone in a strange country, all my possessions gone. No, of course I'm not one of you; on the other hand, could I be more one of you?"

"The men don't like you," Kate persisted. "What's worse, they don't trust you."

"Well, I am not going to turn any of you over to the Protective men, if that's what you mean," Beau said.

Kate was silent for a long moment, staring down at her hands. "Perhaps not." She looked at him, her eyes meeting his unflinchingly. "The men have a word for you, d'Auberge," she said, handing the bottle of rum back to him.

Beau shrugged. "I've heard quite a few," he said, and turned toward the door, thinking it was time to get back to the ship and relieve Ol' Pendeen.

"Then let me ask you a question," Kate said pointedly. "Why do you stay with us?"

Beau shrugged again. "I might ask you why you continue in this trade. You're only going to end up dangling from a yardarm."

"You're not answering my question," Kate said quietly.

"The life suits me—until I have enough gold sovereigns put aside to finish my journey to London."

"I might ease your journey, d'Auberge—but not to London."

Beau stared at her, at her toying, enigmatic smile, and tried to understand what she was telling him, but he could not. "You are the most damnable, confounded woman," he blurted out. "Very well then, ma'am—how would you ease my journey and where would you have me be?"

"I would have you back in your own country," Kate replied peremptorily, sitting upright. "I have often thought of going the America myself. It would be better for me if you were along. As for the first part—" she had grown thoughtful again "—I am not yet quite prepared to tell you that."

"But clearly you trust me more than the others," Beau replied. "Why do you not trust me enough to tell me *how* you will 'ease my journey?' I am not so foolish as to think you mean merely that you have a ship; nor am I so hopeful as to think you admire my person."

Kate laughed, "You are a fine figure of a man, and I would be a liar to my teeth if I said I did not find you so—but no, you're right, that isn't what I meant." She grew thoughtful again, and Beau waited impatiently for her to speak. When finally she did, Kate said very calmly, very steadily, "Did you ever see whales swimming in the open sea?"

She had veered her tack with him again. Although surprised, Beau decided to go along with her. He nodded. "Once, at night. Crossing on the *Loyal Nancy*," he said. "They're beautiful."

"Only from a distance. Up close, they're frightening. They're ugly. Like this shack. Did you know that this place is beautiful from a distance?"

He smiled, thinking she was having another one

of her jokes with him.

"No, I mean it. From my bedroom window at the inn, I can see this place and each morning I look at it. I see this little house all gray from the weather sitting on the sand. It was beautiful from a distance. Do you know why?"

"No, I don't."

"Because it looked free. Isn't that why whales look beautiful? Because they look free, like great, trim ships sailing on the top of the water. They can go anywhere, roam, not care for anything, not having any doubts or fears or pains. Isn't that it? Isn't that why they look beautiful?"

"I guess so," Beau said.

"That's why this shack looked beautiful," Kate said. "Because it looked free. Free from the Revenue laws and free from all people. But just like ships, even the *Gilded Lady*, it isn't really free. Ships are great gray fish with cruel masters and brutal men on their backs. And whales are ugly and dangerous. And this shack is a beautiful little house with a poor drunkard inside it. You see? Up close, nothing is beautiful."

"Some things are beautiful."

"Only from a distance. Up close, you can hear the gears working."

"You're too young to be cynical. You can't bring it off." Beau sat next to her and for a moment he thought he was going to put his arm around her.

"I've been too much in love not to be cynical." Kate got up from the mattress. She seemed tired and her shoulders drooped inside her sweater. For a moment Beau had thought she might fall. He had

122

started to reach out his hand to help her, but didn't. She would not have liked that.

He watched her walk slowly towards the door, pause at the threshold and turn. "It's hopeless, isn't it?" she said, her voice quiet with discouragement. "You dream of London; I dream of America. But they only remain beautiful for us if we keep them at a distance." Her face was full of a sadness he had not seen before and which he did not understand.

"I am careful never to expect too much," Beau said. He folded his arms across his chest and slouched on one hip, enjoying the effect he knew he was having on her. "That's not my style exactly."

Kate nodded sadly, again measuring him in that mysterious way of hers. She turned and walked out the door as Beau moved towards her. When he got to the door, he stopped and watched her walking back to her black mare. He liked the stride of her long, full legs and the slightly circular motion it gave to her pelvis, the rhythmic rise and fall of her full hips. He could see pride in the bearing of her shoulders and that served to make her even more attractive. Women's hips had always held a particular fascination for him and he wondered why that was. He thought perhaps it was because of the way they moved, of the subtle sliding they had. He felt a twinge of disappointment when she mounted the horse, but the continued to watch her until she disappeared into the dust and the distance. He knew he would think about her again that night.

He turned hesitantly back to the shack and then decided against having another drink. Instead, he locked the shack and strode down the beach to the water. It was a long distance back to the ship, and he began his swim with slow measured strokes. He had been gone a long time and as he swam toward the *Gilded Lady*, he hoped Ol' Pendeen would not be too annoyed.

Chapter 11

Kate stood at the window of her room contemplating the small shack where she had last seen Beau, and awaited his arrival. Beyond the shack, across the stand of low lying rocks, was stretched the floor of the St. George's Channel, with a silver-gray film of night mists not yet lifted. A jagged line of cliffs, all projections, dents, bays, and hollows, ran southward till it ended in the great bluff on which the inn sat. The cliff-face was gleaming white, the sea tawny inshore, but the purest blue outside, with the straight sun-patch across it, spangled and gleaming like a mackerel's back.

It was another unusually warm day for that time of year, which betokened an impending storm. Inland, the ground was stubbled with flat stones and divided up into tillage fields; beyond, there was a short sward of open down sprinkled with snail shells. In all, Kate concluded, it was a bleak wind-bitten place enough, looking as if it would never pay for turning the ground. Instead of hedges to divide the fields there were walls built of dry stone without mortar. Behind one of those walls, broken down in places, but held together with straggling ivy, and buttressed here and there with a bramble bush, Kate could barely discern the figures of a boy and girl lying together. Kate smiled, remembering her own fumbling first experiments with love.

The wind had blown fresh all that morning from the southwest and was now strengthening to a gale. Looking up Channel, Kate could see the sky was overcast and the long wall of rock showed gray with orange-brown patches and a darker line of seaweed at the base, for the tide was beginning to come in. There was a mist developing, half fog, half spray, scudding before the wind, and through it Kate could see the white-backed rollers lifting over Peveril Point. All along the cliff face the sea-birds thronged the ledges and sat huddled in snowy lines, knowing the trouble that was brewing in the elements.

It was a melancholy scene and bred a melancholy in Kate's heart. The wind had gone a point or two still more to the south, setting the sea more against the cliff, so that the spary began to fly over the shoal. A fine rain began to fall, forcing Kate to close the window. While she continued to wait for Beau, she passed the time reading the scrap of parchment over again, although she knew it all, word for word.

When Beau entered, he wore a sou'wester and was

dripping with water. "God save us but we're in for a bad blow," he said.

"God save all poor souls at sea," Kate said, glancing up.

"Amen to that," said Beau. "There'll be enough sea on the beach tonight to lift a schooner to the top of it, and launch her in the fields beyond." He walked over to the fireplace where the logs glowed a clear white. "Ah," he said, "I am cut to the marrow with wet and cold and half dead from this damned wind. A fire is a blessed thing"—and he unbuttoned his pilot coat—"and more than welcome now."

They sat huddled in the corner by the glowing fire, the red light flickering on the roof, casting shadows over the handsome, deeply-chiseled features of Beau's face, while steam rose from his drying clothes. Beau drew forth from his pocket a great wicker-bound flask, and offered it to Kate. She took it and drank, not lightly for she had always been a good drinker, then handed it back to him. He put it to his lips, tilting it and drinking long and deep, with a sigh of satisfaction. "Ah, that has the right kick to it. It warms the heart." He twisted the cork back into the bottle and set it before them. "Now then, Kate, why have you brought me out in this weather? I am afraid it's not for the reason I hoped, but I'll hear it anyway."

Kate smiled to herself at this implicit flattery, but was silent for a long while. So long in fact, with her brow furrowed, that Beau felt she was changing her mind.

Beau spoke first. "Kate, pass me the flask. I can hear all the poor folk who ever drowned at sea."

With that he took another long pull and flung a log on the fire. Then, as the light danced and flickered, he saw the piece of parchment lying at Kate's feet. He stretched out his hand to pick it up. Kate would have concealed it if she could, because she had resolved not to tell him how she had come by it. But to try to stop him getting hold of it would only have spurred his curiosity, and so she said nothing.

"What is this, Kate?" he asked.

"It is only Scripture verses," she answered, "which I got a while ago."

For a moment, she was afraid that he might ask her where she had got them, but he merely bantered with her about her new-found religion. The heat of the flames had curled the parchment a little, and he smoothed it out, reading it in the firelight.

"It is well written," he said, "and the verses are good enough. But he was a poor scholar who wrote this, for he cannot give even the right numbers to them. See here, The days of our age are threescore years and ten; and though men be so strong that they come to fourscore years, yet is their strength then but labor and sorrow, so soon passeth it away and we are gone, and he writes 'Psalm XC, 21.' Now I have said that Psalm a hundred times as a boy, verse by verse. I know it doesn't have twenty verses in it all told, and anyway this verse comes tenth—and yet he calls it the twenty-first!"

"How do you say!" Kate cried. "Could you be right?" She spoke more to herself than to Beau.

He glanced at her sharply. "Was this the reason you asked me to come here?"

Kate hesitated no longer, but began at once to tell

Newport

Newport

MENTHOL KINGS

Alive with pleasure!

Warning: The Surgeon General Has Determined
That Cigarette Smoking Is Dangerous to Your Health.

Regular and Menthol: 5 mg. "tar", 0.4 mg. nicotine
av. per cigarette, FTC Report Aug. 1977.

True slashes tar in half!

Only 5 MGS. TAR

TRUE
MENTHOL FILTER

5 MGS. TAR, 0.4 MGS. NICOTINE

TRUE
FILTER CIGARETTES

5 MGS. TAR, 0.4 MGS. NICOTINE

And a taste worth smoking.

him what had happened, how she had thought at first that they were merely verses to protect the dead, but had later come to wonder if there was not some secret meaning to the verses. She had tried to figure out the riddle and had begun to suspect that there was none.

"Is that what you were going to tell me the other day on the beach?" Beau asked.

Kate nodded.

Beau had heard her out patiently, with more of a show of interest towards the end. Then he took the parchment in his hands and read it carefully.

"I believe you may be right," he said at length, "Why should the figures all be false if there wre no trickery in it? If it were one or two which were wrong, I would say some parson had copied them out in error, for parsons are a thriftless folk and would as soon set a thing down wrong as right; but if all of them are wrong, there's no room for chance. Have you got a Book of Common Prayer around the inn? We'll find out one way or the other."

Kate got up without a word and went to a drawer of her dressing table, returning with the Bible which her mother had given her. She sat down again next to Beau and searched out in the book that text about the days of our life, and found that it was indeed the nineteenth Psalm, but the tenth verse, just as Beau had said, and not the twenty-first as it was written on the parchment. And then she took the second text, and here again the number of the Psalm was given correctly, but the verse was two, and not six, as the writer had it. It was just the same with the other three—the number of the Psalm was right but the verse was wrong. Beau had made an important discovery, for it was all carefully written, smooth and clean without a blot, and yet every verse contained an error. But if the second number did not stand for the verse, what else could it mean?

Kate had scarcely formed the question to herself before she had the answer, and knew it must be the number of the word chosen in each text to reveal a secret message. She was in such a great fever of excitement now that she could scarcely count with her trembling fingers as far as twenty-one, in the first verse. It was "fourscore" that the number fell on in the first text, "feet" in the second, "deep" in the third, "well" in the fourth, "north" in the fifth.

"Fourscore...deep...well...north," she read aloud.

So the cipher had been discovered, and what an easy trick! Yet she had not been able to light on it, nor would have except for Beau. It was a cunning plan of Sir Rodger's' but other folk were quite as cunning as he, and here, she felt sure, was his lost treasure at her feet. She chuckled over that to herself, rubbing her hands, and read it through again.

Fourscore...feet...deep...well...north...

It was all so simple, and the word in the fourth verse "well" and not "vale" or "pool" as she had so often struck when attempting to determine if there were a riddle. How was it she had not guessed as much before Beau looked at the parchment?

Kate read it aloud again, and somehow it was a little less clear this time. She and Beau fell to thinking about what exactly it meant. It was hidden in a *well*—that was plain enough, but what well? And what did *north* mean? Was it the *north well* or to the *north of the well*—or, was it fourscore feet *north* of the *deep well?* Kate stared at the verses as though the ink would change color and show some other sense. Then a veil seemed to draw across the writing, and the meaning to slip away and be as far as ever from her grasp.

By degrees, her exulting gladness gave way to bewilderment and disquietude. In the gusts of wind that rattled her window panes, Kate seemed to hear Sir Rodger himself laughing and mocking her for thinking she had found his treasure. Still she and Beau read and reread the parchment, juggling with the words and turning them about to squeeze new meaning from them.

"Fourscore feet deep *in* the *north well*,"—"fourscore feet deep in the well *to the north*,"—"fourscore feet *north of the deep well*,"—so the words went round and round in her head, until she was tired and giddy and fell asleep.

Beau gently picked her up and brought her to the bed and lay her down.

Before he put out the candle, he gazed down at her. She lay on the quilt, relaxed in sleep, her mouth soft and slightly parted, inviting. Beau stood there staring at her until some of the desire in him slipped away to be replaced by a great and aching tenderness. Then, kneeling beside the bed, he kissed her. She stirred drowsily and turned toward him.

Beau loosened the quilt at the other side of the bed, folded it over Kate, then quietly stepped out of the room.

Chapter 12

Lydia stood on the beach a little distance away from Sean and watched the horizon. The *Gilded Lady* rode at anchor in a small cove north of St. Ives, but Captain Maskelyne's ship was not yet in sight. God grant her a safe voyage, she prayed silently, and a speedy return home—to the home of the man who was to be her husband before.... But she stopped her mind before it reached the final thought, and turned to gaze at Sean. Could she bear to leave him? Could that marriage ever be, after what had passed between them?

Sleep that night, she had soon found, was an utter impossibility. Not only had the cold grown more intense during the night, but the very air seemed charged with menace. In the darkness she could hear Susan groaning in her sleep.

Strange how remote Captain Maskelyne had become; once again she was having difficulty in even recalling his face. Suddenly, she felt an arm go around her, and there was Sean looking down at her, smiling. "Are you cold?" he inquired gently.

"Not now—thanks to you." Her tone was much warmer than she had meant it to be; in view of Sean's decision to go along with his sister's plan for ransom and her own uncertainty, she should have been much more reserved.

"Are you hungry? Pendeen should have our breakfast ready by now."

Over an open fire, Ol' Pendeen was boiling cabbage and pieces of ham. In another pot, tomatoes were steaming, while in a skillet thin cakes made of sawdust like flour were baking. Ol' Pendeen saw them coming and grinned widely.

"Come and eat," he called. "tain't much, but 'twill serve!"

Lydia sank down before the fire on the sand, grateful for the heat, and after a moment Susan joined them. Now that she was awake, the older woman looked cold, but Lydia noticed that it did not affect her appetite. Although Lydia had grown used to the strange fare of Sean and Kate and the others, she still tasted it gingerly at first; then, as usual, finding it surprisingly good, ate well. She wondered if she would ever again feel comfortable with the food she used to know. After they had finished, Sean brought them cups of a pale liquor that tasted like beer.

"We make it from fermented meal," Sean explained. "It helps the digestion."

That may well be, Lydia thought, but after having downed half a cup, she realized that it also helped the mind to giddiness and the heart to levity. For the life of her, she was unable to keep from smiling as she looked at Sean. This was a very sorry state of affairs. She forced the corners of her mouth down, but they persisted in creeping up again. Sean's frown deepened.

Why in the name of heaven, thought Lydia, *can't I stop smiling?*

Sean's thoughts at that moment were black and troubled. Captain Maskelyne should be here by how, he thought. He dreaded the thought. But Lydia would come back! Once the ransom was paid and Kate had her money, Lydia would then return of her own free will. She must come back! She was so lovely, this little one, so soft and so tender. And she was his—*his*! He must hold on to that. Never forget her, never. With her eyes that slanted upwards at the corners, her hair like spun silk and her skin like warm mild. No, he would never forget her who lay close to him and wept out her despair; would never forget her. He got up abruptly and looked up and down the beach.

Lydia stood up and took a step or two behind him. As Sean turned, she nestled against his chest, her shoulders shaking with quiet sobs. At long last, she was quiet and raised her small oval face. Suddenly, he put down his head and kissed her. It was a gentle kiss, light and loving, filled with the tenderness which comes after desire. She stood very still with her eyes closed, her mouth warm against his. Then very slowly she moved away from him, her eyes studying his face.

"Say you don't want me to leave, Sean," she whispered.

"When Kate has her gold, you can come back to me, if you still want too, and we'll be married," he said.

"Tell me again, Sean," she murmured. "Tell me what I want most in all the world to hear."

Slowly he shook his head and gazed at her. "You know how much I love you," he said at last. "You know how much this parting is against my will...Come, let us go aboard the ship now." He put out his hand and she took it, her face still averted, tears glistening in her eyes.

"Don't cry," Sean said. "It will soon be over and you will come back to me."

She whirled suddenly and faced him, turning her back on the white sails of the brigantine moving softly on the water. She put up both her hands and let them rest very lightly on his broad shoulders.

"I am betrothed," she said slowly. "You should not have made love to me, Sean. You should not have let me do it. I love you and always will. But if Captain Maskelyne will have me, what can I do?"

Sean looked down at her, bleak pain in his eyes. "You must not say that," he said. "You must not even think it!"

Lydia looked up at him, her eyes bright. "Then wish me God's speed," she whispered. "I would not have us wait for all the world!" Then, rising on tiptoe, she kissed him. He could see the tears on her face. When he released her, he stood looking after her as she walked away, her slim shoulders shaking.

135

Then he, too, walked toward the *Gilded Lady*, feeling with a curious sense of finality that never again in life would he know either happiness, or certainty, or peace.

Sean stood at the rail of the *Gilded Lady* with Lydia and Beau and watched Captain Maskelyne's great ship *Hesperides* inching her way over the horizon.

"Here he comes," Beau said, satisfaction in his voice.

Sean said nothing. He watched the *Hesperides* beat in with majestic deliberation across the St. George Channel. In all the confusion he felt, there seemed to be only one certainty. Sean glanced down at Lydia, seeing the girl's face pale and set, her mouth held in a hard line, her green eyes unwavering. Lydia looked up at him and put out her small hand.

Sean took her hand and held it. His lips broke into a slow smile. Goodbye? Is that all you have to say to me?" he asked, wanting to prolong the moment of their parting.

"Yes—what more can I say? This way is better, isn't it? That we pretend there was no yesterday. We may never see one another again."

"And Maskelyne? What of him?"

"I do my duty," she said simply. "If he will have me now, I must go to him. If he will not, then I will have my heart's desire."

"I see," Sean said.

"Do you? I shall go to Penzance and there I will be a good and dutiful wife to a rich and important man.

And I shall spend all my days in forgetting you. And there will come an hour when I shall succeed in the attempt. Do you know when that will be, Sean?"

"No," Sean said. "When will it be, Lydia?"

"The day I die," she whispered.

Beau touched Sean's arm. "He's coming in now," he said. "Better get Lydia and her servant on shore until this business is over."

"Yes," Sean said. "Emlyn will take them ashore. Then I'll meet this murdering bastard face to face."

Lydia turned and joined Susan and the two of them followed the wizened little Welshman across the beach to where a steep path led through the thick brush that nestled at the foot of the cliff. Sean looked after them for a moment, then turned back to where the *Hesperides* beat through the white wall of surf toward the pale-gold sand.

He and his company, which consisted of Beau, Ol' Pendeen, Dumas and the new navigator, Tomlison, disembarked from the *Gilded Lady* and walked down to the water's edge.

Without hesitation, Captain Maskelyne stepped out into the water, not troubling about his black kidskin, buckled shoes or his fine trousers. From the air by which he carried himself, Sean knew at once that here was an opponent to respect.

John Maskelyne, though not so tall as Sean, was well above middle height, a compactly built man whose body even in repose suggested enormous strength. Beneath the sleeves of his coat, his arms were as big as Beau's and his shoulders broader than Sean's. His nose jutted boldly from his stony face and his chin was heavy. His eyes, brown and deep-set under his heavy brows, rested quietly on Sean's face.

"Where is she?" he demanded in an even tone.

"First let me see the color of your gold," Sean said in an equally calm tone.

Maskelyne leaned forward, peering intently into Sean's face. "I have seen you before," he murmured in a puzzled voice. "But where?"

"Many times," Sean told him, "over the barrel of a gun. And you shall see me again when I am not bound by a safe conduct to spare you. But enough of this. Where is the money?"

Maskelyne nodded to one of the scarlet clad marines who accompanied him. The man stepped forward, grunting under the weight of an oak chest. When it had been opened, the dull glow of gold pieces of gold gleamed in the sunlight. Sean picked up a few of the heavy coins, minted in London from a single heavy bar of gold, and all of them so roughly cut that he knew them to be new.

"Fetch the woman," he said to Beau.

All this time, Maskelyne's eyes had never left his face. On the captain's face was an expression less of anger than of regret—a look of baffled pride oddly conmingled with admiration.

"You are as I should have expected you," he said. "I almost regret that the next time we meet I will see you in the assize."

"I'll see you sooner in your grave!"

Maskelyne shrugged resignedly. "That the cub roars and has fangs I should have known," and he sighed, half to himself. Then his brown eyes lighted, for Lydia was coming down the beach, her face pale and colorless, her lips unsmiling, her eyes cast down to the ground.

Sean watched Maskelyne sweep Lydia into his great arms. A slow, deep feeling of sickness curled in the pit of his stomach. He noted with some satisfaction that Lydia turned her head slightly aside so that the Captain's kiss just missed her mouth.

"He has not harmed you?" Maskelyne growled.

"And if I had?" Sean snarled.

"You would die," Maskelyne said simply. His tone was quite empty of emphasis or of any quality of threat. It was as though he were discussing the weather—a statement of fact.

"No, John," she said quickly, "he has not harmed me. Except for the abduction, he has been most courteous.

Maskelyne studied Sean's face, as though to inscribe it on his memory. "You have your gold. Have we your leave to depart?"

"Yes," Sean said. "Depart and be damned!"

A slow smile played across Maskelyne's dark face. "We shall see upon whose soul damnation will fall," he said quietly. "Come, Lydia." he turned, still holding the girl loosely in the circle of his embrace.

Sean said not a word; instead he turned back to his companions and said very softly: "To the *Gilded Lady*. There is work to be done."

The *Hesperides* was still on the horizon when the winches of the *Gilded Lady* drew her anchor free of the water. The white sails unfurled beneath the yardarms, dropping downward until the light breeze bellied them out and the great fore-and-aft sail on the mainmast filled, the boom swung far over.

Effortlessly, the sleek brigantine began to move out of the harbor.

"Kate did well," Beau said to Sean. "On these last two voyages we've gained more than on any four previous ones." He was wondering how long it would take before Kate's thirst for gold would begin to slacken.

Sean did not answer; he was peering at the *Hesperides*, drifting almost motionlessly on the sun-filled sea. Then he knotted his brows.

"Yes," he said softly, "but we have not yet brought our treasure home. Pendeen, look!"

Ol' Pendeen squinted against the light, following Sean's pointing finger with his gaze. "The son of a whore," he yelled.

Toward the end of the harbor twin lines of war vessels were converging, each coming from opposite directions, from behind the long blue fingers of the mountains. From one side, four ships of the line came; from the other, three. Quietly he called Dumas to his side.

"Crack on all sail," he ordered. "Gunners to their stations."

"If we could gain the open sea," Pendeen groaned, "we might have a chance. Bottled up here, we're doomed: What good is the *Lady's* speed in this deathtrap of a harbor? We'll have to stand and make a fight of it."

"If we can force them to break that line . . ." Sean wasn't sure they could.

"They're not fools," Ol' Pendeen snapped. "The trap was well baited and better sprung!"

Dumas came up of the forecastle and faced Sean.

"Begging the mate's pardon," he began, "I have an idea."

"Then speak, man!" Sean muttered.

"Them ships draw twice and three times the water as us. Now if we was to put back into the harbor, they'd have to come in after us. Inside, they'd run aground as sure as there is a hell—leastwise, enough of them to let us out."

Sean shook his head. "Ships of the line, Honoré," he said. "They mount basilisks and long culverins aplenty—with chaces of sixteen and twenty feet. They could stand out so far that only our one basilisk could hit them—and what good would an occasional hit with a fifteen-pound roundshot to us?"

"From that distance they couldn't throw heavier," Dumas argued.

"Yes, but how many could they hurl to our one? Even fifteen-pound shot will smash the *Lady* to pieces if she's hit with one every ten seconds."

"But if we go out they'll lay on a broadside with sixty-four-pounders—full cannon. Four shots like that can sink us. Suppose we were to lie low and wait for night. In the darkness, perhaps... well, just maybe."

"It's our only chance," Sean said. "But pray God there's no moon tonight."

At Dumas' shouted order the helmsman came about on the whipstaff, and the *Gilded Lady* pulled parallel to the line of Royal Navy vessels. Then she pulled all the way about and headed back into harbor. The helmsman put her about again, and she started a slow glide across the harbor, again parallel to the Navy ships, but in water so shallow that they could not follow her.

Now was the time for action, Sean knew. If the Navy ships were manned by good seamen, they would destroy the *Gilded Lady* in a matter of hours. All they needed to do was to close in until their immensely long and slim basilisks and long culverins were in range and they could pound her to pieces, entirely without risk to themselves. Those long guns threw a very small shot, but they hurled it by such an immense weight of powder through such long barrels that they could outrange guns throwing shot of almost six times greater weight. The *Gilded Lady* had only one such gun aboard, mounted in her bow as a chase gun; the seven Navy ships could muster among them more than fifty. If the ships of the Royal Navy came in before night, the brigantine was doomed.

But to Sean's immense relief, they did not break their line. The continued to patrol the entrance to the harbor with majestic deliberation, crossing and recrossing the open mouth of the cuplike declivity between the Cornish hills.

Dumas ordered a ration of rum to give the men courage, but neither Sean nor Ol' Pendeen touched it, and even Beau, whose taste for the brew was well-known, barely sipped it as he stared at the Navy ships. The day dragged on. The sun burned blood-red on the western horizon. Imperceptibly, it dropped to the water's edge, laying a track of orange and scarlet across which the ships of the Royal Navy crawled like black water spiders. The pastel-blue of the mountains became pale violet, then royal purple, then they lay night-black against the bloody blaze in the western sky. Sean could see the ropes.

"Point-blank range!" Sean roared, and the gunners lifted their hammers, knocking the elevating quoins from beneath the tracks of the guns. As the wedge-shaped pieces of hardwood fell free, the muzzles of the guns dropped until they were pointing at the water line of the reeling ship. The rest of the ships stood by, unable to fire their guns for fear of hitting their own ship.

Again Sean gave the order to fire, and the broadside boomed out, shaking the sea. Plainly, through the echoes after the fire, Sean could hear the crash of the ship's timbers and the screams of her dying crew. Then, to his amazement, a glow of fire showed amidships of the vessel. He could see the figures of men running about on her deck, trying to put the fire out. This fire, Sean saw at once, was a stroke of ill luck, for what illumination the moon had so far failed to give was now provided by the blaze. The *Gilded Lady* lay in the middle of the English fleet, etched starkly against the dancing flames.

At once the Royal Navy opened up with their great cannon, splitting the night asunder. Sean could see the yellow tongues of fire probing the dark for the range, then afterward sea and sky opened with the slow, rolling bellow, the echoes reverberating endlessly among the encircling cliffs. White geysers shot up about the *Gilded Lady* while she fought back, giving them shell for shell. Such was the accuracy of her fire that after the first few minutes not one of the English ships remained unhurt. But

143

the Royal Navy was getting the range now. A blinding explosion of fire, water and oak splinters filled the air not ten yards from where Sean stood. He saw four of his gunners crumple like broken dolls beside their pieces, the pale scrubbed surface of the planking running thick and red with their blood. Beside them one of the demicannon had overturned on its carriage, lying grotesquely on its side with the wooden wheels still spinning.

The *Hesperides* veered into a parallel track and swept the decks of the *Gilded Lady* with a hail of small shot. When she had passed, less than half the brigantine's crew were on their feet. Sean saw Tomlison sitting on the deck, his linstock flaring beside him, trying desperately to push the pink sausage rolls of his guts back into the gaping wound in his belly. He sat there a long time, pushing desperately with both hands, not uttering a sound, until at last his hands were too slippery with his own blood to manage the job. Then he let his intestines spill out and sat staring at them stupidly, an expression which did not change on his dark, swarthy face even after he died. It was only when a forty-eight-pounder hit the *Gilded Lady* squarely, causing her to roll and sending him over limply on the deck, that Sean knew he was dead.

"Mother of God," Sean muttered, "why don't they sink us and get it over with?"

But the Royal Navy continued to slash at the brigantine with small shot, killing her crew one by one until less than two dozen men remained on their feet, and of these not one was unwounded. Beau and Sean were only slightly hurt, cut in five or six places by flying splinters. The helmsman was dead, hanging over the whipstaff, so that the trim vessel veered aimlessly, losing steerage, wallowing helplessly in the sea troughs while the English men-of-war went by her one by one in a beautiful line and raked her decks.

Sean heard at last that most hideous of all sounds to a seaman, the splintering crash of a broken mast; then almost at once the sound of another, so that the *Gilded Lady* lay denuded of her white wings, unable to gain headway. He looked around at Ol' Pendeen, blackened like himself from head to foot with gun soot. Only the flesh about their eyes showed white, streaked here and there with the rivulets of their own blood and sweat. Sean put out his hand and Ol' Pendeen took it. He stood there with the young man whom he had followed and counseled and guided on so many previous voyages, waiting for the death that both of them knew was imminent. And in looking into Ol' Pendeen's eyes, Sean saw no fear.

It was a long moment before either of them realized that the English had ceased firing. They turned as one man, peering through the deafening silence to where the gigantic bulk of the *Hesperides* bore down upon them. The huge ship of the line rose in close and the grappling hooks dropped into place. Sean saw Captain Maskelyne, splendid in his scarlet coat, climb down to the deck of the *Gilded Lady*, followed by a score of soldiers. Of Sean's men, there was not one left with either the strength or the will to oppose them with any effective action.

Stiffly, Sean and Beau and Ol' Pendeen advanced to meet their enemies. The moonlight glinted blue-silver on the muskets and white on the cockades. Sean glanced from the trim uniforms of the Royal Marines to the broken bodies of his dead, tired, sooty wounded. He burned with the rage and humiliation of the moment.

Captain Maskelyne's big white teeth showed in his dark face. His big hand came up and gave his chin a contemplative tug.

"You fought well, my piratical friend," Maskelyne said. Few captains I know could have stood us off for so long. But now we will see if you are so fortunate in the assize."

"Words!" Sean spat. "Do with us what you will, and have done with it!"

"Don't be hasty. All that will come in its own good time," Maskelyne said calmly. "For the moment I will require the ransom money from you. Where is it?"

Sean's eyes glared in his soot-darkened face. He nodded to Ol' Pendeen. The old man started off and returned after a few moments with the chest.

"Open it," Maskelyne commanded.

Sean's tired, stiffened fingers worked clumsily with the lock. When at last it was opened, the gold pieces glinted dully in the light of the moon.

Maskelyne nodded, satisfied that all the money was still there. "Take it up," he said to one of the marines. The man bent and grunted under the weight of the chest.

"Sergeant," Maskelyne continued, "take some of your men and see to it that the dead are buried and the wounded are cared for." Then he turned back to Sean. "Now, if you will order your men aboard my ship, I will have the pleasure of personally putting you in irons."

Sean and the other able-bodied men went up the ratlines to the *Hesperides*. He let himself be led down the splintered, deck, slippery with blood, moving stiffly, his eyes blank and unseeing.

The long line of the men-of-war set sail, moving slowly, silently past the place where one of their ships blazed, bloodying the sea and the sky with the ruddy glow of the flames.

Chapter 13

Snow, light and feathery as puffs of dandelion, was falling in the prison courtyard when, after securing the middle of their ankle chains to their belts with strips of rag, Beau and Sean and the other prisoners started for the courthouse. Days' old beard darkened their jaws.

Lining the narrow, snow muffled street stood a band of youngsters. School books under their arms, they sniffled in the cold. They surveyed the line of blue-lipped men tramping along between red-coated guards. With Dartmoor Prison only a few miles away and with French prisoners of war arriving almost daily, this sight was becoming too common to hold their interest long.

The prisoners passed a detail of grenadiers from His Majesty's Fifth Regiment. Beau watched them pass, boots squeaking on the snow, white-gartered legs swinging in unison. How big they looked bundled in their gray greatcoats! They had tucked their chins deep into high, upturned collars, but their hands looked red and stiff on the brass shod butts of the six-foot Tower muskets. A breeze, whipping the black bearskin coverings of their shakos, wrought fleeting designs, like wind on a laprobe of animal skin.

"It is going to snow harder soon," Ol' Pendeen predicted. "When high gray clouds like that come pouring down from inland, they'll be plenty."

Nobody paid any attention to him.

It was pleasantly warm in the courtroom. Beau looking about, realized this with a sense of surprise. After spending so many days in Plymouth jail, one forgot there were such things as soap, hot water, clean linen and beds. In grim amusement he stared at his hands. Could these really be his hands, with black crescents of dirt under each broken nail? He looked sideways at Sean, then suddenly squirmed. God's teeth! Because of the heat, the lice in his clothes were becoming active. As it warmed, Sean's body began to exude the smell of flesh long unwashed. Sean noticed it himself and looked so apologetic that Beau grinned.

"I'm no rose myself," he said.

149

On the benches sat three judges appointed to adjudicate their case. The grim, hawk-faced presiding justice looked frightening impressive in scarlet robes and a snowy wig.

The court cryer called for order and began reading a directive to the court:

"By his Excellency Thomas Pryce, Governor of Devon, to the Honorable Frances Harrow, Paul Tompkins and Charles Sewall, judges of His Majesty's Court of Vice-Admiralty:

"Whereas Captain John Mackelyne, Commander of His Majesty's sloop of war called the *Hesperides* by his humble petition to me exhibited, setting forth that the said John Mackelyne in pursuance of his duty against His Majesty's enemies did on, or about, the 12th day of December last past, attack, seize and take a certain vessel called the *Gilded Lady* belonging to one Katherine Penhallow, a subject of His Majesty residing in Moontide in the Shire of Cornwall, laden with divers goods and merchandizes and contraband arms, and hath brought said same ship and lading into this port of Plymouth in order of adjudication and condemnation. And by said petition hath further claimed and delivered to this court a sum of monies, gold said to have been paid to the accused in ransom of one Lydia Paddock. Further, by said petition hath prayed for a Court of Admiralty to be holden for trial at the courthouse upon the charges exhibited by John Mackelyne, Commander of His Majesty's sloop of war the *Hesperides*. The officers, mariners and marines belonging to the Same.

Against

A certain vessel called the *Gilded Lady*, the property of a British subject one Katherine Penhallow, and also against all and singular, the cargo and lading on board. Her tackle, apparel and furniture whatsoever, and against the officers and crew of the aforesaid vessel.

Officers attending: Wm. Woolfolk, Marshall
Peter R. Paxton, Register
Ed. Raleigh, Cryer

Given under my hand and the Public seal of this Shire this 18th day of December, 1805 in the 41st year of His Majesty's reign."

Once the cryer had done, some further spectators were admitted. Judge Sewall donned a pair of steel-rimmed spectacles. From behind their square lenses his cold gray eyes deliberately wandered over the double row of defendants.

Judge Harrow glanced at his colleagues, then cleared his throat. "Have you finished reading the charges, Mister Cryer?"

"I have, M'Lord."

There was a brief rustle of papers from the bench, then the chief judge began to speak in succinct tones.

"Pursuant to the laws of England, I do now charge that the owner or owners of the vessel and cargo and contraband taken as aforesaid, or persons concerned shall now appear and show cause (if they have any) why said vessel or any of them and their cargo and appurtenances should not be condemned."

Faggots burning in a big iron stove behind the bench made a noise like distant musketry while the Prosecutor made his plea.

Beau listened with eyes fixed on the Royal Arms rendered in oak. The carving was secured to the wall just above Justice Harrow's snowy wig.

As a speaker the Proctor for the defense left much to be desired; his voice droned on and on like the rumble of a mill wheel. Beau's eyes wandered from the Royal Arms to the back of a marine standing nearby. Between his shoulder blades his scarlet tunic bore a greasy mark caused by the Macassar oil from his queue.

Captain Maskelyne of the *Hesperides* stated his version of the affair in blunt, nautical terms. The brigantine, he swore, had made desperate attempts to evade capture and had opened fire.

A lieutenant of marines, being next sworn, described his boarding of the brigantine. Firmly, he maintained that the cannon aboard the *Gilded Lady* had been charged with ball.

Judge Tompkins interrupted observing that it was odd that a peaceful merchantman plying the Spanish trade should find it necessary to carry cannonades. Was there any explanation?

There was, Mr. James promptly replied for the defense. Said arms and ammunition had been left over from the time when the brigantine sailed in the Jamaica trade. That the justices patently disbelieved this was all too obvious, and there was a murmur of protest from the spectators who were sympathetic to the contrabanders, being themselves much opposed to the heavy excise.

Again and again Justice Harrow rapped for order, but the people occupying the back benches kept up their muttering. Public sympathy came to a climax when the First Mate of the *Hesperides*, striding up to the stand, testified to seditious utterances made by the brigantine's officers and crew. In his opinion they were, the lot of them, traitors down to the soles of their feet, and their contrabanding gave succor to His Majesty's enemies by reducing the tax monies available for the war against the French.

During the noon recess the prisoners were herded into a room adjoining the court. It was empty of furniture. As soon as the door had slammed to, the youngest of the contrabanders began to blubber.

"None of us ever goin' see Cornwall again! We'll get transported or it's the moor. See if we don't!"

Sean for the first time was looking worried and Ol' Pendeen's dried apple of a face was the picture of discouragement. As for Beau, he had never thought there was a chance to odds—and died on the gallows or under the lash. There is no shame in death on the high seas when a man goes down with all guns blazing. I am proud to go that way, and with you."

Without a word, Sean took the old man's hand. While they stood wordless together, the *Gilded Lady* moved out of the harbor with the wind quartering off her stern. And there in the silver blaze of the moonlight the vessels of the Royal Navy waited.

"Hold your fire," Sean commanded, "until we are too close to miss. We will take at least one of them with us tonight."

Cannily, the helmsman held the brigantine in the lee shadow of the mountains, sailing her dangerously inshore, so that before the English saw her she was among them. She slid into line so close to one of the great vessels that a stone could have been hurled from one deck to another without great effort. Sean's hand came down, and all of the *Gilded Lady*'s port guns spoke at once, making bass thunder, every shot going home.

Sean saw the ship's masts crashing down, bringing with them a wild tangle of sailcloth and ropes, and for a moment he began to hope that they might escape. On the impact of the recoil the guns leaped back to the limits of the breech the black-crowned silhouettes of the trees against the deepening blue of the night. The sky darkened until they were drowned in night, blackness upon blackness, and the stars rode the bosom of the sea.

Beau had turned to Dumas to relay an order when he heard Ol' Pendeen's groan. Above the reappearing edge of the mighty cliffs, the great pale yellow disk of the moon was rising. It grew brighter. The trees stood out again, crowned in silver.

Sean looked around him, seeing the twin fingers of the mountains running down darkly to the sea, the black-trunked trees bending seaward before the southerly winds, whistling down across the bay toward where the dark outlines of the vessels passed and repassed in the moonsilvered night, as patient as death.

154

What a night on which to die, Sean thought. Turning to Dumas, he said quietly: "Crack on all sail, Honoré, and hurry the men."

Ol' Pendeen came up to Sean and put out his hand. "You're a fighter," he rasped proudly. "I have seen many who bowed for their release, but he was utterly appalled at the hopeless ineptitude of Mr. James' defense. Why, dammit, the mealy-mouthed bastard was not fit to hold a real lawyer's wig bag!

During the early afternoon Sean and Ol' Pendeen gave their testimony. Firmly they avowed they had not known there was any contraband aboard and that they were merely restoring Miss Paddock to her former financé and that there had been no ransom involved. Lydia's silence and determined refusal to attend the assize had come as a surprise to all but Sean. But even with her refusal to testify against them, their disclaimer succeeded in intensifying the blank expression on Judge Harrow's face.

"Is it not true," demanded Mr. Atherton, Proctor for the prosecution, "that the officers, as well as the owner of a vessel, are expected to know the exact nature of any cargo carried by them? Is it not the law that *all* merchandise must appear on the manifest? Is it not only a master's right but his duty to refuse to sail with an improper cargo?"

Ol' Pendeen got angry and his chains rattled loudly when he spring up and attempted to reply.

"Silence! The prisoner will not interrupt." Justice Harrow's gavel thumped heavily.

Mr. Atherton made an obsequious bow. "Your Honors, the facts are as I have represented them. These men were transporting a cargo of contraband, if not upon this voyage, then upon previous ones. Further, they held one Lydia Paddock for ransom, despite that lady's refusal to come before the court, and this was done at the instigation of the woman Katherine Penhallow, owner of the vessel and presently at large."

His voice rang in every corner of the bare and musty smelling courtroom. "On behalf of His Gracious Majesty, I implore you to find the charges against these men justified. Further, I hold that the owner, Katherine Penhallow, has *in absentia* also been found guilty of smuggling and forcibly detaining one of His Majesty's subjects for ransom."

Mr. James made a perfunctory gesture for dismissal. It was quickly overruled.

"Your Honors!" Ol' Pendeen struggled to his feet. "May I speak?"

Justice Harrow's slash of a mouth thinned ominously, but he ended by nodding.

"While it is entirely true," Ol' Pendeen began in a low-pitched voice, "that I and the other officers engaged in contraband and the ransoming of of Miss Paddock, it is also true that we misrepresented the nature of the cargoes, not only to the crew of the *Gilded Lady*, but to her owner. The owner, gentlemen, is Mr. O'Donnell's half-sister."

Marines surrounding the prisoners glanced side-wise, looking at him from dully interested eyes.

"The prisoner may proceed," snapped the presiding judge.

"I beg of you, your Honors, to dismiss the other prisoners. They are innocent of any illegal intentions. The fault is mine and that of the other officers, but principally mine, because I led the others into these deeds."

Ol' Pendeen stood erect, a grimly unkempt figure outlined against the whitewashed wall. Everyone was looking at him. The scratching of the court clerk's pen continued.

"Your Honors, I beg mercy for these men, if you may find none for me," Ol' Pendeen went on, gripped by an unfamiliar eloquence.

The Justices, like the public, were turning to one another and whispering.

Beau was astonished. He had never heard the old man cut loose like this before. He thought for a moment that Dumas was going to protest this "confession," but then he seemed to realize that their guilt was a foregone conclusion and that they may as well protect as many of their mates as they could. He felt vaguely disturbed. What would the old man say next?

"Most of these men have families, who will suffer through no fault of their own if you find them guilty." Caught up in the swing of his peroration, Ol' Pendeen prolonged it. It was a glittering moment. Even the *Hesperides'* officers were looking at him. Finally, may I say that our employer, Miss Penhallow, is a most loyal subject of His Majesty?" Ol'Pendeen drove home his main point with triumphant emphasis. "That, your Worships, is why I did not inform her about the cargoes. She would never have allowed such aboard her vessel."

Justice Tompkin leaned forward. "Are we to understand, Mr. Pendeen, that Miss Penhallow was innocent of any involvement in the charges against you?"

Ol' Pendeen flushed, glanced unhappily about, seemingly unnerved by the conviction which his words had carried. "Why—why—yes!" he stammered.

An ironic smile broke through the impassivity of Justice Sewall's granite features. "Indeed? Then it is more the pity that she was not a good enough mistress to make sure of what her ship carried." Tallest of the judges, he leaned to the right, whispering with Justice Tompkins. Their powdered wigs lingered close together.

Uncertainly, Ol' Pendeen sat down. He was conscious of the grateful regards of the crew. Sean looked quite amused and bent his head towards him.

"Look at that damned Maskelyne! He looks as though he's fit to spit nails. It won't—"

He broke off as the judges gathered their robes and retired to deliberate.

As the judges rose, all in an instant there came a change in the temper of the spectators. The tumult among the public benches grew so uproarious that grenadiers armed with blunderbusses went back to quiet it. Sean swallowed hard. Plague take it! Whatever the sentence might be, he had already ruined Lydia's life. Maskelyne had said clearly enough that he would not have her. With her silence she had given him the last help she could. And what could he give her, even if he were given a light sentence—the hand of an ex-convict in marriage? What woman would let herself accept that?

In Beau's opinion the deliberation of the judges appeared ominously brief. Within ten minutes the jurists entered, resumed their places. Judge Harrow peered the length of the now stuffily hot courtroom, then cast a glance out the windows. A furious snow storm was raging. He cleared his throat and passed a sheet of paper down to the bailiff, who took it with the air of a man assured of his own importance.

A stillness descended, impressive in its completeness. The bailiff had a bad cold but all could hear him read:

"Verdict of this court. We do unanimously find the charges against the *Gilded Lady* brigantine of Moontide, Cornwall, to be a true bill. She is hereby condemned, together with all her cargo, tackle, furniture and appurtenances whatsoever. Proceeds of the sale shall be divided as prize money among the officers, marines, and mariners of the *Hesperides*, man-of-war, according to the rules and regulations heretofore prescribed. Because of extenuating circumstances, we hold Katherine Penhallow acquitted of criminal intent and exempt from further prosecution. We do find Sean O'Donnell, captain of said vessel, and Yeo Pendeen, mate, guilty of firing shot at a ship of the Royal Navy. The other officers we find guilty of a conspiracy to violate the laws of England upon these two counts: the removal of goods from foreign lands to this, without payment of the excise, and the holding of one of His Majesty's subjects against their will and for the purpose of extorting monies."

Other members of the crew were catching their breaths; they were like men expecting to be doused with cold water. Two or three of them had shut their eyes and the youngest was clasping his hands in an agony of prayer.

"— We do hold the remainder of the crew of said vessel guiltless of willfully transporting illicit cargo; but, as a warning, their personal property aboard the vessel condemned is hereby forfeited. They are hereby discharged!"

"Innocent—innocent!" The youngest sailor leaped up, dirty hands outspread. "Oh, thank you, my lords! Thank you!" He doubled up weeping. The boatswain sat still, staring straight ahead. Though slow to comprehend, he at last broke into incredulous smiles. The man sitting next to him said, "What in hell would you be grinnin' at? How in hell are we goin' to keep warm? How are we after gettin' back to Cornwall?"

"Stow it, you sea dogs!" A beefy sergeant major in charge of the guard turned such a menacing face upon them that they fell quiet.

"There will be no further demonstration." Justice Harrow's voice grated like a knife over a whetstone. "Remove the discharged prisoners."

When this was done and the clatter of chains had subsided, the bailiff blew his nose as loud as a battle bugle and sang out:

"The prisoners will rise and approach the bench and hear the sentence of this court!"

Hands tightly gripped before him, Beau obeyed; somehow the drama of Ol' Pendeen's little speech had completely evaporated. The irons on his legs felt extra heavy and he became overwhelmingly aware that he was very hungry and cold and dirty.

The presiding Justice faced, not the prisoners, but the spectators. Beau's finely chiseled face had gone

160

bronze-yellow and his lower lip became pinioned between his teeth. If he got a long stretch, whatever would become of Kate? Deep inside of him he prayed.

"Grant, O Lord, that I may not appear to be afraid in the face of mine enemies. Lord, I heartily repent my sins. You know that. Move the heart of this Englishman to mercy. Amen."

"—As a warning to other disaffected, dishonest subjects of the Crown, and as an example of the fate awaiting such, this court herewith sentences Sean O'Donnell to twenty year's penal servitude at hard labor at His Majesty's prison at Dartmoor and to transportation from this province to a destination later to be decided—"

The Louisianan leaned forward a little, staring at that vivid splash of robes beneath the royal coat of arms. He cupped his hand to his ear as if he could not hear Judge Harrow's ringing words.

"—In view of the prisoner Beauregard d'Aubege's American nationality, the court is disposed to be generous. But —" Blood rushed through Beau's veins "—we do find you guilty of criminal acts against the English Crown. However, in view of your nationality and the fact that, like the previous prisoner, you have not been convicted of any prior offences, the sentence we impose shall be the most lenient within the power of this court. We do, therefore, sentence you, Beauregard d'Auberge, to serve ten years at hard labor in His Majesty's prison at Dartmoor and to transportation to the country of your birth."

Beau sat down. He had been expecting much

worse from those pale-faced gentlemen on the bench. Still, ten years was a long time to be away from Kate. He smiled faintly; perhaps because of Ol' Pendeen's speech, Kate would be allowed to come and visit him in prison. What bothered him most was whether they would transport him back to New Orleans. Would he have any choice in choosing his destination?

The remaining officers of the *Gilded Lady* stood in a ragged semicircle.

"In view of your previous high crimes and misdemeanors against His Majesty's Government and against the laws of the sea, as are practiced by all civilized nations, as well as acts against the person and safety of one of His Majesty's subjects, this court hereby sentences you to be taken from the jail at Dartmoor on the morning next, paraded through the streets for the edification of the populance, and finally to be put to your deaths in such manners as may be determined. And may God have mercy on your souls!"

The silence had thickness and texture. It could be felt. Every man in the court drew in his breath and held it, none daring to be the first to let it out. So it was that Ol' Pendeen's husky croak had all the carrying power of a musket shot.

Silence then—heavy as death. Then the uproar, complete and terrible from the back benches.

Justice Harrow commenced to collect documents scattered before him and Judge Sewall mechanically straightened the lace at his throat. Judge Tompkins turned to the bailiff.

"The prisoners will be removed to His Majesty's

prison at Dartmoor, there to wait the further instructions of this court."

Ten years, if he lived—Beau thought—of chains, loathsome food and dirt. Beau shivered. What a fool, what an utter stupid ass he had been to meddle with these people. It would be 1812 before he was free again. What city would they transport him to? To New Orleans? New York? Boston? Almost certainly one of these. The realization slowly came to him how long a year was.

"Come on, you." A guard let his musket butt drop on Beau's toes.

Chapter 14

They had left in the morning, a cold, wet morning.
Despite the drizzle and the earliness of the hour, they
found themselves surrounded by drunken sailors out
of the grogshops, trulls with voices like knives, old
women carrying jugs of ale and baskets full of cakes,
fried eels and boiled sheep's heads, by Devon
farmer's in corduroy breeches, red vests that
dropped halfway down their fat thighs, and little
tight brimless yellow caps like the scooped out half
of a pumpkin.

Some pitied them, others did not. "Look at 'em!"
a hag screamed, pointing at Beau and Sean, "loo' ee
at 'em, sayin he's an American, when there ain't
nobody as don't know Americans has red skins."

The English sailor with her looked at her gravely,

raised her chin with his forefinger, and hit her square on the jaw. She went down in a heap in the mud. He swayed on his feet drunkenly, wagging his head at the fallen woman. "Sportsmen!" he said. "Tha's what we are! Treat prisoners like sportsmen even if they be a lot of damned smugglers and the murderers of good seamen."

They had stood about for an hour before their escort of moon-faced Devonshire militiamen started them off at last, up the steep streets of Plymouth and away from the sour smell and the mud. As they went, a piercing wind roared down the abrupt roadways, rain beat into their soggy garments, and brown rivulets of water wriggled from foothole to foothole in the clay-like mud.

Beau expected when they reached the top of the hill to march over a level plain to Dartmoor. But they toiled up the hill only to find that they were at the beginning of another range of hills, somewhat less green than those near the ocean. And when they had labored up the second range, they found a third before them, brownish and sad-looking, drenched with rain and wreathed in ragged veils of fog. Beyond the third, they found themselves still at the foothills of another range, and so it went all through the length of that sullen, endless day. The hills mounted before them, so that the road was like a never-ending river of mud pouring down from some monstrous reservoir high up among the dirty scud of cloud and mist and rain.

The color of those hills changed gradually from brown to gray, and then to a dark gray, so that the countryside was as somber as it was cold and wet.

There were no trees or shrubs on that vast expanse of rolling moors, and no houses—only here and there, at wide intervals, a hut that seemed to shrink into itself at the threatening hills that frowned upon it. As they went higher, there were patches of snow and a biting dampness in the air, the like of which Beau had never felt before.

In the afternoon, they came to the longest of the long hills, its top lost in a driving flurry of snow and rain. There were stupendous granite pinnacles and knobs jutting from its dingy surface as though an angry God had pelted it with the leavings from the rest of the world.

There was a confused babbling from the pie-faced Devon-soldiery in front of them, and Beau caught the word "Dartmoor."

When they had topped the hill at last, Beau found himself looking over a countryside faintly like the one through which they had passed, and yet unlike it. It was more gigantic, as though they were seeing what they had already passed through, but seeing it magnified or distorted by weariness and hunger or a sick man's dream. The ground before them swept off into a broad valley, and then up to tremendous remort heights, treeless and houseless, and dotted here and there by fingers and spikes of granite, small-seeming things in that enormous brown expanse. The road, emptied of all life and un- sheltered by any tree or house from the driving rain and the snow-laden wind, stretched off ahead of them like a dirty string.

The valley and the distant hills were almost black, except where snow lay on them. The drab soil around them, when Beau kicked at it with the toe of his boot, was not good clean dirt, but a slimy black peat, unhealthy and decayed.

They were like black insects, it seemed to Beau, crawling up the roof of a great black barn, insects that might be blotted from the face of nature with little exertion and no regret.

In the late afternoon they came to a wretched square stone house, rising from pools of water in which sad ducks paddled. Beyond it, he saw another, and beyond that a bend in the road and a downward path to a shallow, desolate valley where there were more houses.

Beyond the houses, sprawled against a dingy hill slope, lay a circular mass of granite; a sort of giant millstone.

The cartwheel shape of that dreary place was such that the outer rim of the wheel was stone wall a mile in circumference and twelve feet in height; and thirty feet from it was the inner rim of the wheel: a similar wall, twelve feet in height. Around the top of each wall was stretched a wire to which bells were hung. If any part of the wire were touched, no matter how lightly, the bells set up a clamor, and every guard in hearing came running with his loaded musket. Jutting from the inner rim, at intervals, were loopholed bastions, so that the guards within could sweep the entire prison yard with their musket fire and cut down any person who might be trying to mount the wall and make good his escape.

This enormous tilted cartwheel was divided into equal parts by a high stone wall running through its center. On the one side of the wall were offices, guardhouses and storehouses. On the other side were the prison buildings, seven of them, each one shaped like a huge barn; but their walls were built entirely of stone, and all of them pointing inward to a common center, like clumsy spokes in this vast wheel. The seven buildings were again divided, three being in a yard by themselves on one side of the semicircle, and three in a yard on the other side. In between, standing alone and walled off from the three on the right and the three to the left, was Prison Number Four, which was the deepest and darkest in the place, barring the Cachot or Black Hole itself where the most truculent and intransigent of the prisoners were kept.

The high wall that separated the prison half of the millwheel from the other half was pierced in the center by a high barred gate. The gate led from the prison half into a market place, a hundred feet square, which might be regarded as the hub of the wheel.

They were herded like sheep beneath a stone archway in the outer wall, taken in hand by a detachment of kilted, bare-kneed Scotsmen, and driven down through the inner gate and into a small stone house that stood on their left, near the hospital. Their clothes were soaked and coated with mud. There was mud in their hair and some of them, like Ol' Pendeen, could not stand upright because of the blisters on their feet.

Beau and Sean had only the dimmest recollection of their first night in Dartmoor Prison; because when they were sure that the men would have food and a place set apart for them to sleep. Beau seemed to move in an ever-thickening haze of drowsiness, a haze that pressed against him as heavily, almost, as water, and when his head dipped beneath its surface, as it often seemed to do, he knew nothing, though it appeared he was able to walk and talk and even eat a little while so submerged. He recalled passing hordes of half-clad Frenchmen, and coming among more black men than he had ever seen together except on Mambo holidays in New Orleans. Above all else, he remembered the tumult, for none of these prisoners were sitting quietly, but were engaged in trades and traffickings, tending small shops, crying their wares, peddling their products, crowding around gambling tables, or operating miniatures restaurants and coffee stalls.

It was early in the morning, after what seemed an age-long night of waiting, amdist fitful bursts of sleep, that Beau and Sean were rousted from their beds and herded out into the courtyard with the other prisoners. There was a distant throbbing of drums as the prisoners marched in file to the center of the square. Now it would begin. Now the men who had followed Kate for so long, the men with whom he had lived and fought through gun smoke, would die—ignominiously, ingloriously, terribly.

When Beau and Sean reached the square with their cell mates, the square was already packed and they saw at once that all the preparations had been completed. The executioner took his time. At the foot of the gibbet the kettle-drums never ceased their thrumming beat. Now they quickened as the first of the men was led to the scaffold. Step by step the bo'sun mounted upward accompanied by a black-garbed minister and two stout guards, and at every step the drums cried out, gloating.

Beau tried to turn away his eyes, but he could not. There was the blare of horns, the roar of gunfire, and a mighty roll on the drums. Then silence. And black between them and the sun, the grotesque pendulum swung, amid a stillness so great that its very creaking could be heard.

The crowd which had come from their houses scattered over the moors to watch the executions was roaring now, hoarse-voiced, demented. The bo'sun was followed by the navigator, Santiago, walking proudly on the scaffold. Beau was sure he heard the bone snap even above the shouts of the crowd. In the echoing silence after the bellows of the crowd was stilled, two figures creaked gently at the rope's ends, their necks bent far over in that terrible angle which has no counterpart in life.

Despite his proud beginning, the little, bandy-legged Spaniard had died badly. He had to be carried the last few steps to his death, making hideous noises in the O which had formed of his mouth. Now, at last, Beau found the strength to turn away. When he looked again it was not yet done. The little Spaniard's weight was insufficient to break his neck from the drop, and he hung there kicking, his swarthy face purpling slowly, until two soldiers, moved by some strange compassion, caught both his legs and swung downward with all their force.

Then they brought out a Frenchman. He had been stripped naked and his body was a magnificent thing, rippling with superb muscle, bull-throated, deep-chested, great of limb and thew, like a statue carved by some ancient Roman. Reluctantly, Beau had to acknowledge to himself what Kate had once seen in the man.

Four red-coated soldiers hurled him flat on his back on a rack, and the cords were tightened about his wrists and ankles. Beau saw the executioners place their poles into the sockets of the winch and turn it slowly until the sweat stood out on the swarthy body as Dumas was slowly stretched until every major bone had been dislocated. Then the chief executioner stepped forward. In his hand he held a long, limber rod of iron, no thicker than a man's thumb. Now, slowly, lightly, with apparent grace, he began to strike the Frenchman, and with every blow that landed with easy, dull regularity, a bone was broken.

Beau could hear the Frenchman's low, deep-throated grunting become louder, change into a heavy moaning, until at last the man's heavy legs tore apart and he loosened his last, piteous dying screech. When they cut the cords, he was a sponge-like thing, lacking entirely in rigidity, so that when the soldiers picked him up he folded over in their grip like a doll stuffed with cloth.

The hot tears stung at Beau's eyelids and seeped down onto his face. His face was ghost-white beneath his tan. So that was how Kate's mother had died, how Kate herself would have died, if her men had not remained true to the smuggler's code and refused to tell on their companions. Suddenly, weakly, he bent his head down and retched on the ground. Sean put his great arm across his shoulder.

"Courage, Beau," he whispered.

171

The drums picked up their rolling again. This time it was different—a slow and solemn beat. Lifting his head, Beau saw a platoon of soldiers with a minister walking slowly to one side of them, reading silently from a Bible. Among the soldiers, stumbling blindly, so beaten, whipped and tortured that his bruised and branded face was almost unrecognizable—Ol' Pendeen. He was not led to the gibbet; instead the soldiers led him to a pock-marked wall, which up to now Beau had not noticed. Beau had to grip Sean's shoulder hard to keep from falling. Sean was looking away, the tears running down his cheeks.

The executioner made short work of binding Ol' Pendeen to the iron pole which stood in front of the wall. The blind was applied. Ol' Pendeen seemed too numb to care, but at the last moment his mouth came open, and clear above the angry crackle of the rifles, Beau could hear the inrush of breath as he gulped air into his lungs. His head went back, pressing against the iron pole, and the red maw of his mouth showed plainly, his lips drawn back from his yellowed teeth. But the scream never came out. Clearly, cleanly, across the courtyard the rifle shots awakened echoes endlessly reverberating, and Ol' Pendeen hung limply against the pole, a dark, spreading stain blossoming on his ragged shirt front exactly above his heart.

"He died well, Beau," Sean said.

When the investigation failed to turn up any concrete evidence against her, Kate set furiously to work. It had been necessary to arrange a transfer of funds to a bank in London, funds upon which Lydia

172

could draw during her efforts to secure a pardon for Beau and Sean. Gradually, Kate had watched those funds begin to dwindle as it proved necessary to bribe one petty official after another. Nevertheless, without Lydia's well-connected family in London it would have proven impossible for Kate to even begin to make the effort to free her brother and Beau. Poor Lydia! How cruelly she had been rejected by Captain Maskelyne after he had effected her "rescue." Kate smiled to herself. Thank God, Captain Maskelyne had formally renounced the engagement before the assizes were in session. If he had not, Kate wondered, would Lydia have borne witness against Beau and Sean and herself?

Despite her thoughts, Kate's pen, flying over the account ledgers, never ceased its busy scratching. What was Beau doing at that moment, she wondered. She shuddered to think about it. She forced her thoughts back to the figures which she was tolling up in a neat little column. She had a good business head and would prove it again on this occasion, which was probably the most serious financial crises she had faced since taking over the running of the inn after her brothers' death.

Nervously Kate raised her eyes to the little square piece of paper which lay in the upper right-hand corner of her desk. She gone cold the moment the bailiff had begun fumbling in his coat pocket. Too well she had guessed its contents; too much had she inherited of her father's sound business instincts. Her stay strings had then seemed made of wire; an irresistible force drew them tighter, tighter. Once she had had a return of the old dream of climbing the rigging and being carried off by a huge bird. Now she felt the same sense of panicky helplessness.

As she opened the envelope, Kate remembered how the small snarling noise of ripping paper had sounded like the crack of doom and of how she had read, the tips of her fingers pressed to her lips:

Katherine Penhallow, Prop.
Respected Lady

Yr. Vessel being now seized by His Majesty's government in most unfortunate circumstances we feel justified in exacting paym't for marine fittings and supplies delivered per yr. order to Vessel *Gilded Lady*, October last.

Demand herewith the paym't of all sums of monies due and accrued Interest, or Land or Merchandise to that value.

Yr. humble ob't serv't,
Andrew Lydgate.

Now of all times! With her monies committed to buying the freedom of Beau and Sean from some corrupt Lord of the Admiralty, why did all this have to happen now! Almost any day she expected to hear that Lord Tyrone, one of the most powerful men of the Admiralty, had acceded to Lydia's pleas—for a "consideration," of course. But what had become of Lydia? She had not heard from that young woman since a week previous.

When she had first seen the lonely figure wearily trudge up the windy headland, his hat pulled down against the bite of the sea breezes, she had thought he might be bringing news from Lydia. When she recognized the figure as that of the bailiff, her heart had sunk.

When she had first read the note from Mr. Lydgate, Kate's expression had hardly changed at all; then a nerve had begun to tick in her cheek. Next a big vein had begun to swell on her temple and to stand out like a blue cord under the skin. As she reread the demand note, her hands began to shake.

In a queer, strained voice, far more alarming than any burst of temper, she said aloud in a thick voice, "He must be crazy!" She wanted to think so, but she knew very well that Andrew Lydgate was not given to making any kind of error.

She flushed scarlet. For the past two weeks she had been expecting to be pressed by her creditors, as soon as the news of the *Gilded Lady* had gotten about. She had been preparing explantions against this moment, but now she couldn't think of a single one.

The day's accumulation of irritations and that persistent sense of impending disaster combined to stir her into a blind fury. The hound dog cringed, slunk back into a far corner of the kitchen and peered fearfully from a corner of his eye.

In an abandon of misery, Kate started blindly toward him. She reached for a thong to punish the dog; then she hesitated. She felt that she was regaining herself, but instead a white light broke in front of her eyeballs and the crack of the thong drew a frightened whimper from the dog. Giving the animal a look of contemptuous hatred, Kate walked into the dark.

Near dawn she had gotten into bed and made a

rigid pretense of sleeping.

At this moment, however, Kate put these memories out of her mind, picked up her pen and resumed entering her figures in the inn's ledger. She stopped, erased an incorrect figure with a knife blade, then used a piece of deer's horn to burnish the rough spots. The cold did not make it any easier to enter the figures correctly. Besides, she had not been feeling any too chipper in the weeks since the capture of the *Gilded Lady*. In the mornings she woke up feeling logey, heavy; to get breakfast was a terrible chore. She was deeply grateful that Reverend Castallack had sent some of the village men up to help her with the really heavy work.

Chin on hand, she rested, peering on the long rows of cottages in the village and the steeple sprouting behind them. She resolved that she would invite the Reverend Castallack to visit her. He would be a great comfort during the long winter evenings.

Chapter 15

When Beau thought about what it was which weighed heaviest on his spirits in the life at Dartmoor, he unexpectedly found it difficult to say. One moment, he convinced himself that it was the stench of the place—the bittersweet, flat, choking smell of unwashed bodies and fragments of food and hidden filth. At another moment, he thought it was the cold. The windows had no shutters, only iron bars, so that the bitter winds, the daily rains and snows, and the penetrating fogs that curse Dartmoor for nine months in every year poured in on them day and night.

At other times he convinced himself that it was the despairing rage he felt at the outrageous wrongs inflicted on them by the guards—inflicted not because they had committed wrongs but because of the amusement which such actions afforded their jailers. At still other times, Beau thought it was the fear, the uncertainty as to their fate. In ten or twenty years, for all they knew, they might become forgotten men, be kept in that dripping tomb for the rest of their lives, unless they could escape. And this was not a grandiose fear, for on every side of them were Frenchmen who had rotted there for years, despite the temporary peace, forgotten and forsaken by their country, their families, and their friends.

Still another source for the despair which pervaded his bones each minute of each waking day were the fleas. They lurked in the cracks of the floor or the folds of their hammocks, creeping out at night to feed on their bodies, raising welts which kept them awake in torment with their burning and itching. Strangely, the lice did not bother Beau so much. He kept his body and clothing as clean as he could and remained relatively free of them. But the fleas were different. They were too quick to be easily caught, and cleanliness was no protection against them.

Still another cause for his malingering despair was the constant threat of disease: smallpox, typhus and pneumonia. Or the clamminess which soaked up from the floors through their bones. Or the manner in which the guards taunted and jeered them. God knows, they got more back than their thick wits could have thought of, but that was little solace, Beau found, for a man who knew himself to be a prisoner regardless of his ready wit.

After they had been there a month Beau had conceived a plan of escape. In a few weeks, there was

178

a detachment of Frenchmen scheduled to be exchanged for English soldiers which the French held. Beau had spoken French since childhood, and although his Southern accent might be detected easily by a Frenchman, it was scarcely likely that their guards would. Sean, however, was another problem. Although he proved a quick learner, his Celtic accent, half-Irish and half-Cornish, proved an almost insurmountable problem. Another problem was to find a friendly guard. Between them, they had sufficient funds, but they could not afford to mistake their man.

Having decided to hold their French lesson each day away from the other English-speaking prisoners, for fear of being too closely questioned, they went daily to the French barracks, across the stone-flagged yards, slimy from dirt, and the unending moisture of the Dartmoor mists. There, swarms of yellow-clad prisoners were walking, gabbling, yelling, playing childish games and working at various pursuits while waiting for their noontime soup to come from the copper boilers in each prison's cookhouse. It was here that Beau and Sean sat each day with their backs to the inner prison wall and while away their hours speaking French.

A small canvas bag of coins dropped into Corporal Timothy Malloy's hands, wrought the miracle.

"Here's half," Sean had told him. "You'll get the other half when we're delivered. And don't try any tricks on us, soldier!" Sean scowled. "Or you'll have your heart cut out on duty some night." In the dim light, he looked really ferocious.

"Faith then, 'tis meself will be careful."

When the day at last came, the market-square of Dartmoor Prison was a busy place. All the petty shopkeepers among the prisoners were in constant need of replenishing their stores of tobacco, pipes, needles, thread, awls, boots; pots, pans and pails; butter, eggs, cloth, coffee, tea, beer, rum, meat, fish, soap, and God only knows what else. But on this particular day it was busier than it had ever been. Not only were patches of blue sky showing now and again through the low-lying fog bank that hung perpetually over the prison when rain was not falling, so that the market folk were out in full force, but the news of the prisoner exchange had brought scores of visitors to the prison. These were the friends and relatives of the French inmates who were being congratulated on their release.

Against the side walls of the square were rails to which were tied the donkeys of the market folk who had ridden in from Tavistock and Widecombe-in-the-Moor and Moretonhampstead—donkeys that added to the turmoil by bursting into brays so mournful that they might have embodied the hopelessness of all the remaining prisoners.

The market folk were ranged behind long trestle tables set in a double row down the center of the square, while the richer merchants occupied the choicest positions, close against the barrier between the market place and the prison yards. There they could easily carry on their traffic in obscene toys with the French prisoners, giving smuggled brandy and dirty books in exchange for the toys. Usually, they had purchased this advantage from a prison

180

guard, but some had to scramble for their positions at the opening of the market, while the prisoners pressed against the railings and cursed them for the manner in which they crowded the women of the prison out of the way, sometimes even oversetting them and trampling on them in their anxiety to snatch the most desirable places.

On that morning there were more prisoners than usual packed along the railing between the prison and the market place. Prisoners were peering from the end windows of every prison house and crowded on the prison roofs. The first draft of French prisoners, five hundred of them, were passing through the iron-studded gates and down the road toward Plymouth. Beau and Sean both turned their heads away from their window. If there is a sight to make a man sick and desperate, it is to see others march away to freedom while he stays behind.

It was not until the third draft that the corporal came walking down the cell block. His heavy tred echoed hollowly amid the damp silence.

"A fine evening it is," he said, peering through the little barred window cut into the wooden cell door. Quickly entering, he set down his musket. "Hold out yer feet, sor."

Heart pounding, Sean obeyed.

Corporal Molloy made a deft selection of the keys: the gyves fell away.

"Now you, sor." Molloy crossed to Beau and the red cloth of his uniform was briefly bright in the shaft of sunlight which fell through the window. Two keys clicked and another set of gyves lay like useless serpents on the bug-infested straw. Molloy might have been doing nothing more dramatic than unlocking a woodshed door. Clearly, this was not the first time that Molloy had set prisoners free; it was probably a very lucrative sideline for him. But it was lucky he was calm, Beau thought. Sean was shaking like a colt the first time he smells a bear.

"Plaze to come wid me. Niver a noise now," pleaded the Irishman. He wheeled sharply about and picked up his musket, marching them ahead of him as if he were on guard.

The keys on Molloy's big ring clinked a little as in single file the three men trooped along one faintly reverberating, stone-walled passage after another. Then down two stone stairs, gritty with dirt. Running rats. Doors and bars, bars and doors. A sour unclean reek of dirty human bodies. Prisoners snoring, muttering in uneasy slumber. Loose straw sticking from under doors.

Beau and Sean had let their beards grow for three days because seen in the confusion of the courtyard at the moment there was always a chance they might be recognized. When the draft was called they took their hammocks and bags and went out past the sentries, Molloy walking guard behind them, and into the market place, wearing the patched yellow rags they had bought from Frenchmen.

Because of the persistent outbreak of smallpox, many prisoners who had died were not marked down as dead and the prison records were badly kept. For years, the prisoners had drawn the rations issued to these dead men and sold them, and drawn clothes and shoes in their names and sold them; and then, having no further use for the names or to pay their gaming debts, they sold the names as well.

The names they had chosen, Pierre Marie Claude Barthes and Jean Paul Renard, Molloy told them, would be called together, probably in the third draft.

It had all been so easy. For the first time since he could remember Beau felt an urge to weep. The let-down was too great. The nightmare was over—or promised to be. The unbearable monotony, the dirt, the hunger, the lice, the gnawing fear of that moment when he and Sean would be dragged away for transportation to God knew where.

"Walk ahead," Molloy directed softly and they caught up their small bundles. "Ye will plaze walk in a straight line like prisoners. Take yer place in line and bejabber wid no one."

Molloy, walking behind, herded them along.

They watched the Frenchmen ahead of them in line pushing up to the gates at the far end of the market place, eager to be gone from the mud and fog and dripping walls of Dartmoor. Clerks at the gate, already bored by the hundreds of French names which had gone before them, took the names of those who passed out, checking them off in a ledger.

It is the waiting, as every man knows—waiting and thinking of what might happen—that causes more men to fail in crisis than almost anything in the world. It was to shorten this waiting that Beau turned to look for the last time on the angry stone faces of the seven prison houses. For a moment he had the illusion, indeed, that they were faces, grotesques that gnashed their teeth at him. Upon the roofs stood lines and clusters of prisoners, following them hungrily with their eyes when they trooped through the gates. Other prisoners were pressed against the iron barrier at the far end of the market place, as Sean and he had pressed themselves to their window to watch the first draft of prisoners go out.

Before they knew it, almost, they were marched through the arched gate and out onto the slippery road. The long line prisoners stretched so far down the hill ahead of them—the hill at the bottom of which lay Princetown—that the head of the column was lost in the mist that had come to seem as much a part of Dartmoor as her fleas and the bells on the wires around the walls.

Beau had long looked forward to the day when he should find himself on the outside of those iron-studded doors; but now that the dream had become a reality, he felt only a profound depression at the thought of the thousands of men who remained behind.

Beau turned and looked back, up the hill toward the prison walls. There were four guards at the end of their long column. Strung out behind the guards were baggage wagons, loaded with the duffel bags of the prisoners. Nearer to them were the guards, few in number, who walked alongside the column. Twenty or thirty paces behind Beau and Sean, walked Molloy. He had certainly demanded his pound of flesh for their freedom and, at first, Beau had not liked him. But now that he was almost free, he felt differently; he decided that the little Irishman had merely driven a hard bargain, but, by God, he was following through on it loyally.

The road itself was a trench cut into the slippery black peat of the moor. He and Sean looked desperately about for drains into which to crawl, but there were none. There was only the barren river bed of a road, slimy with mud. They looked for thickets in which to hide, but the land was without grass or trees and the film of fog was beginning to lift; a desolate rolling expanse, with fingers and humps of granite thrust up through it here and there, but all of them far removed from the road on which they marched. There were no houses. Nothing. Only the vast stretch of black moor, to which an early spring had brought a faint swarthy green, such as Beau had seen come over the face of a black man afflicted with seasickness. The longer they walked and studied the landscape, the more clearly they saw that there was no way for the two of them to scramble from the marching column unseen.

With sinking hearts, they realized they would have to wait until they reached Princetown before effecting the last phase of their escape. They could only hope that the English did not immediately embark the prisoners onto vessels bound for France.

They reached the Devonshire Coachman in Princetown in a sweat of apprehension, for fear they would be overtaken before anything could be done to make good their escape. The line of prisoners had halted and the officers of their guards were standing expectantly near the door. The door opened and some men emerged with a barrel of beer clasped in their arms. A portly, aproned man came out and shouted: "Here now! Doan't jis stand about. Help youmselves!" The prisoners surged forward, forcing Beau and Sean toward the inn. The men seized the keg and drew it toward the middle of the street.

While they did so, Beau and Sean flattened themselves against the front of the inn, near the door, and stayed there, which was not difficult, since all the others sought to be near the barrel.

Another man, this one in a rusty top hat and a long smock emerged from the inn, carrying a stout wooden horse. Two boys very important followed him with a bung starter and a basket of earthenware mugs. They saw Molloy standing in the door of the inn, his arms folded benevolently, a smile on his face, looking at them. Beau and Sean edged themselves along until they were behind him.

They heard the thumps of the bung starter, followed by the gush of beer and the slushy chuck as the spigot was driven home. Sean dodged through the door, and Beau after him. They stood in the stuffy, beery dimness of the inn's taproom, holding their breaths and listening for a cry of alarum, but they heard nothing except the happy, thirsty babbling of the Frenchmen and their guards.

They looked at each other; then, at a slight sound, looked quickly around. In the doorway facing them stood a girl, a buxom, red-cheeked girl in a frilled cap and short-sleeved dress. She nodded and turned away silently, evidently expecting them to follow her. They tiptoed after her, and she led them up three flights of stairs; then stepped aside to let them enter a smelly attic with two pallets of straw in the corner.

There was the sound of a slap and a scuffle behind Beau as he crossed to the dusty small window.

"Don't be a zany!" the girl said.

"But you are so beauty-fool, *ma chérie*," Sean murmured, his eyes appraising her shrewdly.

186

"You Frenchies!" she exclaimed and tittered. "They's clothes under the beds, carter's; clothes. Boots be under pillows. Lay youmselves on them beds, and don't forget ye're droonk. They's rum yonder on that washstand, and if any o' them guards come up, ye be droonk."

Sean scuffled with her as she tried to leave, but she broke away and closed the door laughing. They tore off their yellow prison garb and scrambled into the clothes that lay neatly folded beneath the mattresses: leather breeches, red vests to the thighs, long dust-colored smocks, and worsted stockings that pulled over the knees. Under the pillows were enormous boots and rusty battered top hats, such as every Devonshire wagoner wears. They knew they were not the first escaped prisoners that Molloy had ever sent to that attic.

That night they made their way through the back gate of the inn and out into a street which was very black except for distant whale oil lamps. Before Beau and Sean realized it, Molloy was following a path leading towards the Tamar River.

"Now if the blessed Saints are kind, we'll find your boat and you'll be off."

Hidden among some high weeds and half under a deserted dock they found the rowboat. Once Beau and Sean had each taken an oar, Molloy spoke: "Fine. 'Tis the divil's own pull at this hour. So you'll want to be waiting 'til the three o'clock patrol goes by. The tide'll be down by then." He straightened up from his squatting position alongside the boat and turned away, waving a hand over his shoulder. "Well, the best o' look to ye, boys." Then he was gone.

They waited and sure enough the church bells had scarcely finished their drowsy tolling than a barge came pulling along the shore. It was manned by six rowers in addition to a pair of officers seated in her stern. Beau could see their muskets shine in the light of a lantern set on the boat bottom.

It was wise they had waited. The night was so dangerously fine one could see the tree on the Cornwall side of the Tamar. Millions of stars cast a perceptible sheen over the river. Frogs along the Devon shore grunted and splashed.

Fortunately, just as they pushed off, a small, steady tide began to draw them toward the Cornish shore. The corporal, no fool, apparently had paid attention to details. The rowboats tholepins were cleverly muffled. More important still, the rowboat was equipped with a little leg-of-mutton and a flask of brandy.

Never, Beau thought, had he smelt a sweeter wind. His legs felt unfamiliar without the customary twenty pound weight to them. Absently he reached down and felt his ankle. He had no difficulty whatever in locating calloused ridges raised by his gyves. Small wonder. There was a touch of early spring in the air; they had been there almost the entire winter.

Sean was all excitement. He kept saying to Beau in eager undertones, "Isn't it amazing! We are actually free! Think of it! We can go where we like, eat what we like, drink what we like! By god, I can taste Kate's roast duck right now!"

By the time they had reached the Cornwall shore, they were less than fifty miles from the inn.

Three days after their escape, their pardon arrived from Lord Tyrone. When Kate heard the news of their escape from them, Kate wept—she wept partly to see them free and partly for all the monies she had lost on their pardon.

Chapter 16

The Reverend Castallack stood in Kate's private sitting room by the fireplace, his bald head bent deep in thought. Idly, at first, then with deepening interest, he fingered what must be a set of plans for a new brig. The fact that Kate had drawn plans for a vessel was in itself unusual. Although not a nautical man himself, the Reverend Castallack had spent his life and ministry in seaport towns and had come to know a good deal about the sea and the ways of seamen. He knew for instance that at Liverpool, Plymouth and Southhampton, where the best English ships were built, a shipwright planned his vessel as he went along. He would mount stem and stern posts first, then lay the keel and commence framing out from amidships. Any inspirations

190

would be more or less spontaneous and only then put into execution. What Castallack beheld neatly rendered in India ink caused him to bend his hairless head in admiring concentration.

What with her specifications for pickled and boiled timbers, Kate was aiming mighty high. Imagine calling for copper treenails below a merchantman's water line! Good Heavens! What did Kate think she was building? A yacht! A ship-of-the-line? Tapping his hands softly behind his back, the good man considered the way the brig's prow was to be sheered. Why in the name of all that was holy was she planning to place the mainmast so far forward. Involuntarily, he moved his head in disapproving jerks. Suddenly he recognized her. She was the same ship whose working scale he had seen downstairs on the mantel above the fireplace! So that was how Kate had been whiling away her lonely hours waiting for news of her brother and Beau d'Auberge.

One thing seemed certain. What with that tricky rake to her masts, Kate's new brig was either going to be speedier than a cat with its fur on fire or she would be a miserable failure, a laughing stock wherever she went. If she did prove a success, though, her speed would pay for her in jig time. Ummh. Could be pierced for six guns. The Reverend Castallack hoped Kate was not going back into the contraband, even as she had promised she would not. But what then was the confounded woman up to?

The Reverend straightened hurriedly when Kate reappeared. Her color was high and her jaw set at a stubborn angle.

"Hope you don't mind, but I've been taking a look—" He broke off. Kate's eyes were growing very tense and hard and narrow.

Horses, several of them were advancing up the headland. When Reverend Castallack started up, Kate warned him in a low voice:

"Stay where you are!" Her eyes caught his, asked a number of silent questions. Then because the riders seemed to have halted, she went to look out of a window. Turning, she said over her shoulder, "They've come seeking Beau and my brother."

He made out four riders whose horses were blowing and snuffling in the darkness. One of them swung off, looped the bridle over his arm and led his mount up to the door. The beast shied and the man cursed under his breath as Kate's hound dog suddenly appeared and began a shrill series of yelps.

Kate watched a second man dismount, a big man with a sagging stomach. He wore the uniform of a major in the Royal Dragoons. He began to stomp his feet and the others swung their arms as they sat in the saddle. The leader, wearing a triple-caped riding coat, rapped loudly on the door with his riding whip handle; the gesture irritated Kate no end. What right did he have to come pounding on her door at this hour of night?

Kate felt a little better on recognizing the leader as Major Matthew Henry. A blond, sardonic fellow, he would much rather preach Rousseau's philosophy at the Cock and Bull in St. Ives than tend to his military duties. She remembered also seeing him downstairs at the Carnforth, but she had never encouraged his visits.

"Hello Kate! Will you open up, please?"

"Who is it?"

"Major Henry, Captain Maskelyne, and two more of His Majesty's servants!" rasped the second dismounted man. "Open up or you'll get to hear from some more of us."

"Be quiet," Henry ordered. "I will do the talking here."

Quite deliberately, Kate slid back the oak bars fashioned by the original owner. They were quite stout enough to keep out intruders.

"Evening, Matt. What can I do for you?"

The civility of the greeting surprised the leader into taking Kate's hand. "Evening, Kate. Deuced cold night." He sounded embarrassed and hunched his shoulders nervously under the light gray riding cloak.

"Yes. Reckon sleet will be leaving off soon, though."

Major Henry cleared his throat. "Sorry to disturb you. There have been reports that your brother and another man who used to work for you have been seen in the neighborhood. Not two nights ago. Have they made any attempt to get in touch with you?"

"Why, no," Kate replied easily. "Why?"

The two men on horseback put their heads together, muttering something Kate could not catch. Captain Maskelyne started to speak, but Henry cut him short with a peremptory gesture.

"I hope you will not be deceiving us, ma'am. If you are—well—it would be—" Ill at ease the Major pulled off his hat, studied the interior of it a moment. He brushed a hand over his forehead. His breath, rising in small white puffs, became gilded by firelight beating through the open door. It revealed handsome intense eyes, a tangle of dark blond hair and a wide red scar along his cheekbone.

Kate grinned. "I think this would be the last place that my brother and his friend would come for succour."

Swelling his chest until the polished brass buttons of a new red naval uniform threatened to burst, Captain Maskelyne swaggered forward. Kate could see the coat's scarlet facings and his waistcoat of the same color were peppered with wine stains. He seemed tipsy.

"I warn you, woman. If you're hiding either one of them, or giving them aid in any way, you'll find yourself swinging on the gallows with them."

"You would enjoy that wouldn't you, Captain. Then you could say that you murdered all of the Penhallows," Kate fired back.

A pasty-faced, thin fellow in a dingy red uniform leaned forward in the saddle. He was a corporal in the Fifth Dragoons. He said in a hoarse, passionate voice, "After we had traced them as far as Launceston, we learned that they had come this way, south over the moors. And you say they weren't coming here!"

"But what difference does all of this make? They have been granted amnesty, have they not?" Kate pointed out. "This matter is before the courts at this moment."

"Maybe. But that don't keep us from doing our duty," the pasty-faced man insisted.

Captain Maskelyne's dark eyes narrowed cruelly

on either side of his beaked nose.

"Once a bloody smuggler, always a bloody smuggler, says I. We aim to find them, right, men?"

"We'll find them for you, Captain." The fourth rider who had just dismounted heavily from his horse leaned a long-barreled musket against the inn and began methodically to rub his beast's thick legs. "We'll stretch their necks if we catch them."

"You'll be no better than criminals yourselves," Kate flashed. "Anyway, I haven't laid eyes on my brother nor on his friend."

"You're sure about that?" Major Henry sounded very suspicious.

"Of course. Why shouldn't I be?"

"Captain Maskelyne was waiting on the raod for us. He thought he heard your dog barking at someone, then your door stood open."

"By Jesus, there wasn't no 'thought' about it," Maskelyne growled. "I've got ears in my head, haven't I?"

Kate's diaphragm stiffened when she saw a coil of rope slung to the thin fellow's pommel. It was not a thick rope but it was quite thick enough to hang a man. All four of the wind-bitten riders carried pistols.

"Well, I still haven't seen anybody. What my dog barks at is his business," she said desperately. She wondered how many small groups like this one were out that night hunting Beau and Sean, more intent on sport than justice.

The pasty-faced man uttered a derisive snort and, after blowing on purpled hands, passed his reins to his companion. "Do you want us to have a look around inside, Major?"

Kate stepped into the doorway, filling it. She was angry, but realized that she had better hang on to her temper. "You have no right to enter my house like this," she said in measured tones.

"I'm going to take a look about as well," said Captain Maskelyne in a determined voice.

"Stay out of my house, you murdering bastard!" Kate darted toward him. "You have no authority here." Tight-lipped, she turned on the major, now standing aside, uncertain, increasingly embarrassed. "What ails you Matt Henry? After all your fine philosophy, you allow these men to come to the inn and act no better than highwaymen. If you'd mind your courtesies more and leave your philosophy alone, you might become a gentleman!"

Collecting himself, Major Henry bowed. "Servant, Ma'am. I regret we have disturbed you and so long as you are sure no one is here, we'll be going. Mount up, boys."

"Hold on, Major—" Maskelyne began, but Major Henry cut him short.

"That will do!" he snapped. "You are not aboard your ship now, Captain—and you heard my order!"

"Have it your way this time, Major. But right now, I'm saying I'll soon be riding this way again. Then, my lovely, we'll see if you don't end in Dartmoor along with that other trash!"

The thin, pasty-faced corporal suddenly stopped swinging his arms. He bent forward in his saddle and fixed a steady, accusing gaze on Kate. "Woe unto the oppressor of Israel! Search your soul, Kate Penhallow! Dare you play the role of Jezebel and the

Whore of Babylon?"

Kate merely stared. She didn't know whether to laugh. Maskelyne took fresh courage and slapped the butt of his pistol.

"Let's get a light. What do you say, Major. Your troops have the right to look for a felon anywhere. It says so in the Military Instruction Manual—Chapter Six."

"That may be so." The Reverend Castallack suddenly stepped forward into an oblong of yellow light flooding the frozen ground. "However, I can guarantee you that you are making the greatest mistake of your lives."

"What the hell—?"

"Listen to me, young fellow. As God's minister, I assure you that any deeds you do here tonight will not go unnoticed, either by God or your superiors. So be very careful of your every action."

Even the horses cocked surprised ears at the little, bald-headed minister's booming voice. The riders, visibly impressed, kept quiet, their chilled faces intent.

Scowling, Maskelyne asked in a surly voice, "Then we have your word as well, Reverend, that no fugitive is hidden at the inn?"

"Miss Kate's word is sufficient for me to give mine to you," said Reverend Castallack quietly.

Major Henry laughed quietly and settled his cloak against the west wind's bite.

"Is that word good enough for you, Major," Maskelyne asked angrily.

"I presume it must be. All right, mount up, men, and let's get going."

197

The major had started to swing up onto his horse when, in a nearby tangle of myrtle and holly, sounded a sharp rustle of undergrowth.

"By Jesus, there's one of them!" Maskelyne swung to the sound, jerked out a pistol. "Told you they were somewhere around!"

"There's nobody there," insisted Kate sharply.

"Like hell there isn't!" he said, ignoring Henry's urgent plea. "Don't be a fool!" The sea captain fired at a dim blur in the undergrowth.

Terrified yelping and a violent threshing was the immediate result.

"It's the dog!"

A harsh *crack* sounded as Kate stepped forward and hit Maskelyne, not with her open palm as is usual with her sex, but with her closed fist as she had learned to do from her father and her brother. Startled, Maskelyne stumbled back, losing his balance on the rocks that dotted the yard. Arms flailing, he landed at his horse's feet. Snorting, it began rearing and backing away.

Kate turned to rush inside for a pistol, but ran into the spread arms of Reverend Castallack. For a moment, Maskelyne made no effort to rise, only lay cursing under his breath. Maskelyne raised himself on one elbow and began feeling his jaw. Dazedly, he spat some bloody spittle.

"Give me that pistol you fool!" Captain Henry was roused to a cold fury and when Maskelyne hesitated, he stooped and jerked the second and still loaded weapon from Maskelyne's belt.

Maskelyne only stared at Kate with a malevolent intensity.

"The dog's all right," Reverend Castallack called, returning with the cowed and trembling hound in his arms. He stood straight and serious, but inwardly he remembered the tom-girl Kate had been when she had come to his school as a child, and he felt proud that her spirit had never been broken.

Furious, Major Henry ordered the men to mount up. "I deeply regret this disgraceful affair, Ma'am. My apologies," said the Major once the other men had moved off. Then he spurred his tall chestnut and cantered after them.

Chapter 17

It was about two hours after Reverend Castallack left and Beau was sitting in an attic room mulling over where their lives would eventually lead them, when Sean's brown face appeared framed in the trap door. Beau peered up, anxious. It was turning colder. Maybe he had better give his friend the goose-down quilt off his own bed; once again he had found that two slept warmer than one. "Will you be warm enough, Sean? Take the quilt from my bed."

"Won't need it. It's a damn sight snugger here than in most stern cabins—or prisons for that matter," said Sean grinning. Over the wind's impatient rattling of the window frames, Sean's voice sounded muffled. All of him had vanished up a rope ladder some minutes earlier, through a trap door in the attic ceiling which had been built nearly a hundred years before. "Will you be sleeping up here tonight," Sean added, with a grin.

"No, I don't believe so," Beau said, grinning back at him.

Sean began pulling the rope ladder up. "Good night, then. And thank my sister for those ducks. They were elegant. There's few women that can cook a duck. Most of them cook a duck until it's brown and tough like a parings of the Devil's hoof. Well then, good night." The trap door closed.

"Good night."

As Beau came down the stairs to the main room, a gust of wind shook the whole inn and a leaf blown in under the door skittered across the floor. Beau's candle was equipped with a hurrican globe or it would have gone out. Down on the lagoon a flock of wind-tossed geese, lighting in, evoked a querulous welcome from those already bedded. Tonight their honking sounded eerie, restless. Perhaps Captain Maskelyne and the others had passed that way.

A familiar sense of oppression and of times and people long lost descended upon Beau. He wished he had Kate's capacity to live in the present and prepare for the future. By God, despite her recent turn of events, that little lady sat up nights figuring out how to put her business back together, and with her backside only just out of jail. All of her talk about starting over again in America, her "New World." He thought of his father. His father had been just like that, but then his father had picked a good time to live; life in his day had been simple and uncomplicated. Kate was simple and uncomplicated.

Beau drew a slow, deep breath and frowned. One thing was certain. He would not stand for Kate, no matter how much he cared for her and respected her business ability, grabbing at the tiller of the family politics whenever she disagreed with him. She had as soon learn that now as later. The more he thought about her stubbornness the more indignant he became. What, he wondered, was her brother's opinion of a man who could not even handle his own woman? He would make her understand a thing or two before they blew down the hurricane glass that night.

He lingered in the inn of the kitchen for a few minutes, after having sought her there and not found her. He lingered framing a series of severely polite and inflexible pronouncements then, shading the hurricane lamp with one hand, he sought the main dining room. He found it in darkness, save for the fire's lazy glow. He was pleased that Kate had not yet gone into her bedroom; in there, she had a way of distracting a man's serious thoughts.

Beau drew himself up. "Kate, I want to—"

"Oh, darling." She came gliding towards him. "I thought you would never come down."

"But Kate!" Desperately Beau recommenced, floundered; his pronouncements escaped like mercury through his fingers. All he could think of was Kate. She was standing before the fire but half turned aside. Her face wore an expression of radiant expectancy. He had never dreamed that such a look could have shaped her features when he had first met her. The throbbing coals had deepened the color of her slightly parted, moistened lips. at the same time betraying spasmodic motions of her breasts.

Shutting the oak door behind him, he put down the candle and cried in a thickening voice, "Kate—I—I—Oh God, but you are lovely! So unbearably lovely!"

"To you, always I hope," she murmured. Her eyes dark and softly luminous. Slowly, she parted delicate arms, let her head back a little.

A delicious astonishmemnt seized him; the laces of her bodice were hanging loose and the top of her frilly blouse was slipping low, lower, baring her smooth shoulders. The fire's heat beating on his back passed through his body in a succession of impulses so hot they seemed to warm the palms of his hands pressed tight to her waist. He neither saw nor suspected her small smile over his shoulder.

A man, he frantically tired to remember, should never let his good sense be carried away. How many times since they had first made love had Kate tried to interfere in what he wanted to do—as though she were still his captain; order him about when she had no call—oh hell! He might as well have tried to reason against the sweeping force of a freshet. Moments such as these were unnerving; they were so unexpectedly paradoxical. Until a few weeks ago, he had had no hint that such ardent flames could heat the cooly poised woman who had run the *Gilded Lady* and the inn.

In her bursts of passion she was astonishing. If that wooden mermaid which Ol' Pendeen had carved on the prow of the *Gilded Lady* had left her perch to spin and whirl in a bachanale, the act could not have been more surprising.

"Ah, Beau, my own man," came her heavy, tremulous whisper. She smiled up at him and he could have sworn small fires smouldered in the depths of her eyes. Sometimes back in Louisiana, when he had gone off shooting with his father, he had noticed a similar lambency in the eyes of a hound lying beside a campfire.

When he bent her, passive, tremulous over one arm, the loosened gathering string at the blouse's neck gave way, baring her arms to the elbows. He pressed his face, glowing as though scorched by an August sun, to the deep valley between her high, firm breasts. Light as hovering butterflies her fingers brushed his dark wavy hair and undid the sober black bow clubbing it over the nape of his neck. This was all right, Beau had to remind himself. Weren't they now partners in the venture for the Mohune diamond. He needed no longer to be on his guard against her. He began to speak in a hoarse, urgent undertone.

"I love you, dear, and together we'll build your boat in America and start a new life. If the ship's as fast as you say—we'll soon have a small fleet of merchantmen—and a great warehouse—every-thing—everything!"

Her laugh came softly tender. "Oh, Beau I'll believe in your star—we'll succeed, I feel it. And I'll be content, whatever we do."

Without warning, she whirled away, deliciously disheveled, ineffectually clutching the fallen blouse and catching up the candle at the same time. At the top of the stairs to her bedroom she paused, darting a mischievous look over her bare shoulder.

"How many petticoats?"

Grinning, Beau deliberated. "Let's see. You had three yesterday, five the day before. Four?"

"Right, Mr. d'Auberge," said Kate and blew out the light.

Chapter 18

It was daylight when Kate awoke and the wind had fallen, though she could still hear the thunder of the swell against the rock-face below. Beau and Sean had set a fire to burning in the great fireplace and sat by it, cooking something in a pot. They looked fresh and keen, like men with no troubles in the world, rather than like two men who had been hunted over the moor and must ever afterward remain watchful and uncertain of themselves.

Beau stood up and stopped stirring the pot as soon as he saw Kate coming down the stairs, laughing and saying: "How goes the night, Watchman? You sleep so sound it might have taken a cold pistol's lip against your forehead to have roused you."

Despite the jovial greetings of Beau and her brother, Kate sensed that both men had been engaged in a deep conversation only moments before she had entered the room. She was content to wait through breakfast until one of the men decided to broach the subject of their meditation to her. This Sean did as they repaired to the tap room and Kate poured them each the mid-day tankard of warm spice wine to keep out the chill which still hung in the air. They had decided that they must make still one more effort to locate Sir Rodger's missing treasure.

"It is the only way, Kate, my love," Sean explained. "Even if the court reinstates our pardons, we can't remain about the countryside for another two weeks, and that's for sure. If we're to repair the family fortune, this is the only way. We can't go back into the gentleman's trade."

"No," Kate said, "not now. We have no ship and the risks for us are now too great."

"So let us go over Sir Rodger's dark utterances again," Beau said returning to the fire. "If he means it, let us see what it is he means. First he says it's a well. But what well?"

"The depth he gives," said Sean resuming his seat by the fire, "is too deep for any well in this part of the country."

Kate was about to say that it must be the well at the Manor House, but before the words left her mouth she remembered there was no well at the Manor House at all. The house was watered by a running brook that broke out from the woods above the house, and jumping from stone to stone, ran through the Manor gardens and emptied itself into the tide below.

"And when I come to think on it," Sean went on, "'tis more likely that the well he speaks of was never in these parts at all. For see here, old Sir Rodger was a spendthrift, squandering all he had, and would most surely have squandered the treasure, too—if he could have laid his hands on it. And yet 'tis said by the legend that he did not. I think he must have stowed it safe some place—and afterwards he couldn't get to it. If it had been anywhere about the village, he would have had it up a hundred times. But Kate, you're the one who knows the old stories from your talks with Parson Castallack. So speak up, Kate. Though you've told them a hundred times, maybe it will help us to come to some judgement on the matter."

So Kate once again began to tell the old stories of Sir Rodger and his clan, how Sir Rodger had been a wastrel from his youth and squandered his inheritance on riotous living and was set to guard the King in the castle of Carisbrooke. But there he took a bribe of a rare diamond from his royal prisoner to set him free, and with the treasure in his pocket, turned traitor again and showed a file of soldiers into the room where the King was stuck between the window bars, escaping. After that, however, no one trusted Sir Rodger and so he lost his post and came back in his old age to his Manor House, a broken man. There he rusted out his life, but when he neared his end, was filled with fear and sent for a clergyman to give him consolation. It was at that parson's insistence that he made a will and bequeathed the King's diamond, which was the only thing left of his fortune, to the almhouses in the village. These were the same hospitals that he had robbed and let go to ruin. They had never benefited by his repentance, for when the testament was opened there was the bequest plain enough, but not a word to say where the treasure was to be found. Some said that it was all another of Sir Rodger's mockeries; others that he had never had the diamond; others that the jewel was in his hand when he died, but carried off by someone who tended his last hours; still others that he had buried it in the churchyard; and finally there were those that said it went down with much other fortune at sea. But most thought, and handed down the tale, that being taken suddenly he died before he could reveal the hiding place of the royal diamond and that in his last throes he struggled hard to speak, as if he had some secret to unburden. Kate concluded by saying she thought his secret had died with him because he kept hoping for recovery, hoping that he would be able to retrieve it himself.

As Kate spoke, both Beau and Sean listened to her as though all these tales were new to them, as indeed many of them were to Beau. It was when she spoke of Sir Rodger being at Carisbrooke that Sean made a quick little move as though to speak, but did not, waiting until she had finished her tale.

"Well, for myself, I make nothing out of it," Beau said with a heavy sigh.

Sean said nothing for a long while, but sat buried in his own thoughts. Finally he spoke:

"Kate, the diamond is still at Carisbrooke. I wonder I had not thought of Carisbrooke before you spoke. There you can get fourscore feet and three and four times that much should you want it. 'Tis Carisbrooke, Kate, make no mistake about it. I have heard of that well from childhood, haven't you; and saw it once when I was a boy. It is dug in the castle keep and goes down fifty fathoms or more, down into the chalk below. It is so deep, they say, that no man can draw the buckets up on a winch. They have an ass inside a treadmill to hoist them up."

"But why," Beau interposed, "should Sir Rodger have chosen a well in which to hide his diamond?"

Sean shook his head. "That I don't know. But if he did, 'twas odds he would choose Carisbrooke. 'Twas his conscience speaking."

Sean spoke quickly and with more fire than Kate had known him to use for a long time. She felt he was right. It seemed natural enough that if Sir Rodger were to choose a well it would be the well of the very castle where he had gained his treasure so treacherously.

"When he say the 'well north'," Kate said, "clearly, he means to take a compass and mark north by the needle. At eighty feet in the well below that point, the treasure should be hidden."

"Well, well, well," said Sean laughing at his own joke and clapping his hands noisily, "when will we be off? Tonight, if it suits you two."

"Not you, Sean," Kate said quietly.

Sean stared at her dumbfounded, and even Beau seemed unable to speak. What could be more natural than for Sean to accompany them?

"We have already fixed with the *Bonaventure*'s men," Kate explained, "that they should lie off the coast tomorrow at midnight if the sea is smooth, and take you off to London on the spring tide. How could you have forgotten? Midnight is their hour and we set this with them eight days ago."

Sean's brow furrowed. He had far from forgotten Lydia, but time had passed so quickly. "No, Kate," he said finally, "much as I love the woman and want to see her, that can wait. This venture is more important."

Kate set her tankard on the floor with a little show of force. Beau could see she was angry, but determined not to show what she felt.

"You are not necessary on this venture Sean. Beau will do just as well, and your absence will not make your share any the less—if that's what worried you." The she added in a milder tone. "Besides you will be safer in London with Lydia. I have made all the arrangements. The *Bonaventure* will take you to St-Málo. There you will meet Lydia and proceed together back to London. No one will be searching for you by that route."

"I am going with you."

Beau stirred uneasily in his chair. He did not want to be caught in the middle of a family quarrel, but he sensed one was coming and his own relations with Kate had caught him up in it, made him, however reluctantly, a member of the family. He shuffled his boots on the wooden floor and began speaking slowly, in an effort to give himself more time to think.

"Beau! Kate! This is not, of course, any of my affair and you must each do what you feel is right. But consider, Kate: an extra pair of hands may be needed in this venture. Who knows what problems we are going to find at Carisbrooke? It certainly is not going to be as easy as it seems."

There was a look of astonishment on Kate's face, and with that, an almost hurt expression, as if she had not expected that he, of all men, should be siding against her.

"What difference will three or four days make, Kate," Sean said, hoping to conclude the argument gently. "Lydia can wait that long for me."

"But consider, Sean," Beau went on, "what those three or four days will be like for her Sean. What else can that poor woman think, but that you've been taken—or worse? For us those few days will go all too quickly, but for her—"

Sean bent over, resting his elbows on his knees, staring at the floor. It was clear to all that he was going to London.

"Unless, of course," Beau continued, "we could find some way to get a message to her. But who is there we can trust? If only Ol' Pendeen were still alive."

All three sat for a moment, each involved in their memories of Ol' Pendeen, as though in a moment of silent prayer, then Kate rose abruptly.

"Yes, but he's not," she said. "But there is one we can trust, up to a point. If I gave a sealed letter to Parson Castallack, telling him nothing of its contents, he would see it got to London for me. And no one, not even Captain Maskelyne, would suspect the good man of working hand-in-hand with contrabanders."

"A devious plan, sister," said Sean laughing, "and one not entirely fair to the Reverend. But how like you!" Sean clapped his hands with happiness. "I'll pen the letter within the hour."

Kate flashed a warm, affectionate smile at Beau and thought to herself that Beau was perhaps not the gentleman she had always imagined for herself, but he was a man of quick wit, and with her fortune gone, that was what she needed. Yes, she had chosen well.

"As for yourself, brother, if you are set to go on this venture, and have your mind made up to put your head into a noose, I am not such a loving sister that I will not let you play the fool."

Beau sighed. "Well, then, it's settled. How do we begin?"

"I know the castle," Kate said. "It is not more than two miles from Newport, and at Newport we can lie in at the Bugle, which is an inn addicted to the contraband. The King's writ runs lamely in the Channel Isles and Wight. If we want a safe place, maybe we shall find Newport as safe as St-Mâlo."

Beau and Sean looked at each other and smiled. Having lost her ship had not made Kate any less the captain.

Chapter 19

That next night was well suited to flight. There was a spring-tide with a dark moon and a light breeze setting off the land which left the water smooth under the cliff. They had seen the *Bonaventure* cruising in the Channel before sundown, and after darkness fell she lay close in and took them off in her boat. There were several men on board who knew them all and greeted them and made much of them during the short voyage to the Isle of Wight.

The wind sent them up-Channel and by daybreak they put us ashore at Cowes. They walked to Newport and came there before most of the town was stirring. The few people they saw in the street paid no attention to them, but doubtless took them for two carters and a young woman who had brought corn from the country for the Southampton packet and were about so early merely to get a good start on the day.

When they stopped at the Bugle, they found they had the choicest lodgings and meat and drink and a landlord who treated Kate as though she were a queen. And so she was indeed a queen among the gentlemen of the contraband and all the landers between Start and Solent. At first the landlord would take no money from them, saying he was in their debt and had received too many good turns from the Penhallows in the past. But Kate had some gold which she had received from Lydia recently and finally forced him to take payment.

Beau and Sean were out most of the day, and Kate saw them only rarely between breakfast and supper. They had gone separately to Carisbrooke, and told her that the castle had last been used for men taken in the earlier French wars, but now was empty. King George was now too old and, it was rumored, insane, to make the long journey from London, so that the grounds were unkempt and unguarded and the castle itself guarded only by the retainers who lived there. They resolved to put their plans into action with a moment's further delay.

Sean and Kate had little trouble finding the well-house, having been to the castle as children with their father. They crossed a small court and came to a square building of stone with a high roof like the large dovecots found in old stackyards.

The building was open and the first thing they saw was the treadwheel which they remembered from their childhood. It was a great open wooden wheel, ten or twelve feet across, and resembled a millwheel, only the space between the rims was boarded flat. Treads had been nailed on it to give a foothold to the donkey. At the side of the wheel was the mouth of the well, a dark round opening with a low parapet around it, rising about two feet from the floor.

Kate felt so near her goal. Yet was she near it at all? How did they know that Sir Rodger had meant to tell the hiding place of King Charles' diamond in those words? They might mean a dozen things besides. And if the words did speak of the diamond, how did they know this well was the right one? There were a hundred wells besides. These thoughts came over Kate, making her hopes of a new fortune less sure. Perhaps, she told herself, it was the steamy overcast night or the scant supper they had eaten which beat her spirits down. She knew that people's moods change a great deal with the weather and with food. But she was sure that now they stood so near to putting their venture to the test, she liked it less and less. She felt their every movement was being watched and she could think of no one who would be watching them but Sir Rodger himself.

But neither Beau nor Sean seemed to share her misgivings. Beau had taken the coil of rope off his arm and was undoing it.

"We will let an end of this down the well," he said. "I have made a knot in it at eighty feet. Well, eighty feet below us, when the knot is on the well lip, we'll know we have the right depth.

A spindle ran down from the axle of the wheel across the well, and on the spindle was a drum to take the rope. There was a clutch or fastening which could be fixed or loosened to make the drum turn with the treadwheel or let it run free and a footbreak to lower the bucket fast or slow or stop it altogether.

"I'll get into the bucket," Beau said, turning to Kate, "and Sean here will lower me gently until I reach the end of the rope. Then I'll shout and, Kate, you fix the wheel and give me time to search."

This idea was not to Kate's liking for she had thought that it was she who should go down. She said so. "No, that's not the way to do it. It's my place to go down. I'm smaller and lighter than either of you."

"No, Kate," Sean said quickly. "If the bucket were to break loose, I would have the best chance of climbing back. And I mean that for you, too, Beau. I'm younger and stronger and I would have the best chance to survive."

Reluctantly Beau agreed; he did not think Sean's chances would be much greater than his own, but he was anxious they present a common front against Kate's impetuosity. Finding herself outvoted, Kate was as always, sullen, but contented herself with saying, "Are you sure this well is clean, that there are no deadly gases lurking down there?"

Sean brought another candle out of his pocket, fixed it on a wooden triangle and lowered it on the rope. It was not until then that Kate knew what a task Sean had before him, for looking over the parapet and taking care not to lose her balance, because the parapet was low and the floor green and slippery with water, she watched the candle sink into the cavernous depths. From a bright flame it turned into a twinkling star, then to a mere point of light. At last it rested on the water and there was a shimmer where the wood frame had set the water rippling. She watched it twinkle for a little while and Beau raised the candle from the water and dropped down a stone. The stone struck the wall halfway down and went from side to side, crashing and whirring until it hit the water with a booming plunge. A groan and moan rose from the eddies. To Kate they seemed like those dreadful sounds of the surf which she heard on lonely nights at the inn, when the water glutted the sea caverns underneath the headland.

Beau pulled the candle up and put it in her hand. Then Sean got into the bucket. Kate stood at the breakwheel, and Beau leaned over the parapet to steady the rope.

"Are you sure you can do this, boy?" he said, speaking low and putting a kindly hand on Sean's shoulder. "Are you head and heart sure?"

Sean threw back his mane of golden hair in the old familiar gesture and smiled. "Well, let us find out then," he said.

Chapter 20

The bucket was large enough for Sean to stand in it with both feet. The experience was not entirely new to him, for he had climbed many a rigging in his day, but yet he could not deny he felt ill at ease and fearful when the bucket began its descent into the darkness and the air grew more chilly. Beau lowered the bucket slowly enough so that he was able to take stock of the wall and how it was made. He found for the most part it was cut through solid chalk, but lined here and there with brick where the chalk had fallen away. Slowly the light from above died out and all was black as night except for his candle. Far overhead he could see the well-mouth, white and round like a lustreless full moon.

Eventually he felt the bucket stop and heard Beau

shout something from above, so that he knew he was about eighty feet deep. Holding onto the rope with one hand, he began to look around, not at all knowing what he was looking for, but thinking he would see a hole in the wall or perhaps the diamond itself reflecting his candlelight. But he saw nothing. What made his search more difficult was that there the wall was completely lined with small, flat bricks and looked much the same all round.

Sean examined the wall as best he could by marking a portion with melted wax and turning round in the basket until he had come back to the wax. He tried this method two or three times without success, until he had to give it up because he was beginning to feel dizzy.

He heard Kate and Beau talking together, but could not make out what they said because of the echo in the well. Then he heard Kate shout, "Beau says he thinks this floor has been raised. You must try lower!"

The bucket began to move slowly lower. Sean gripped the rope tighter and took care not to look down into the unfathomable abyss below. When the bucket had dropped some six feet lower, he again began to examine the walls. They were still built of the same shallow bricks, and examining them as before, he could at first see nothing. But as he looked downward his eyes were attracted by a deep scratch on the wall.

The sides of the wall were not moist, green or clammy, like the sides of wells where damp and noxious air have a chance to form. They were dry and clean, and Sean knew that this was because far below there were entrances and exits for the water, so that it was always kept moving. The mark he saw was as fresh as if it had been made yesterday. It was not deeply or regularly cut, but roughly scratched, like boys scratch their initials on stone walls. To any other eye, it would have looked like nothing more than a wavy line. But to Sean it inscribed unmistakably the letter "M".

By holding on to the rope with his left hand, Sean could reach over far enough with his right to touch the wall, but that was as much as he could do. He shouted up the well that Beau must bring him nearer to the side. They understood what he meant, so they slipped a noose over the well rope and drew it to the side and made it fast.

The brick was at about the level of his face. There was nothing to show that the brick had been tampered with. It did not sound hollow when he tapped it, but when he looked closely at the joints, it seemed to him that there was more mortar than usual about the edges. He fixed the wooden frame of the candle to the rope by its chain and began chipping out the mortar with his dirk.

Soon he had the mortar out of the joints. By putting the blade of his dirk in the crack, Sean could prise the brick forward. When he had gotten the brick out, he put it in the bucket in case he needed to inspect it later to see if it were hollow. No sooner had he taken this precaution when he saw the tell-tale glitter of what he sought in the little hole. Three or four small diamonds had spilled out of a small parchment bag. When he had put the loose jewels in his pocket, he brought out the parchment bag which looked like the dried bird eggs cast up on the beach after they have fallen from the cliff nests. Dessicated, these eggs are crisp and crackle to the touch. As a child he had picked them up and found that a pebble had gotten inside them and rattled like a pea in a drum. The little bag he pulled out was also dry and crackling and there was something the size of a small pebble that rattled inside it. But although the bag was parched and dry, it was not easily torn. Only with an effort was he able to rip the corner of it with the sharp edge of his dirk. Then he shook it carefully and a few diamonds fell into his hand, one of them as big as a walnut.

At first Sean could think of nothing but the diamond that had belonged to Charles the First, neither of how it got there nor of how he had come to find it. With such a prize, Kate and Beau could live happily and he would be a rich man able to support Lydia and have the blessing of her family. So he clung to the rope, swaying gently, being filled entirely with such thoughts, and turned the stone over and over again. He wondered more and more as he watched the fiery light fly out of it. He was dazed by its brilliance and the possibilities of wealth which it offered him and, in a way natural to all humans, felt a desire to keep it to himself for as long as he might. In that mood, he thought nothing of the two waiting for him at the mouth of the well until he was suddenly called back by Kate's voice.

"What are you doing? Have you found anything?"

"Yes," Sean shouted back. "I have found the treasure. You can pull me up."

The words were scarcely out of his mouth before

the bucket began to move, and he went up a great deal faster than he went down.

As he neared the top, he heard what seemed to him a third voice speaking, but he could not make it out amid the hurried conversation and the echoes of the well. But just before his head was level with the ground, the break was set and the bucket stopped where it was. Sean was glad to see the light again, but irritated to have been brought up so quickly and then stopped. He looked up and saw the face of Captain Maskelyne, who was pointing a pistol firmly at his chest.

Holding one pistol on Kate and Beau, Maskelyne was leaning over the parapet. He placed the pistol in his left hand on the parapet and reached his hand out to Sean, saying, "Where is the treasure? Give me the treasure!"

By stretching out his arm, Sean could have placed it in the captain's hand, and was just about to do so, when he caught his eyes and something in them made him stop. He refused to hand him the jewel until he was safe out of the well. Sean felt certain that as soon as Maskelyne had taken the diamond, he meant to let him fall down and drown below.

So when Maskelyne reached down his hand for the second time and said, "Give me the treasure," Sean again answered: "Pull me up then; I cannot show it to you while I am standing in the bucket."

On that Sean whipped the diamond back quickly into the little parchment bag and thrust it into his breeches pocket, meaning to have a fight for it, anyway, before he let it go. And looking up again, he saw Maskelyne's hand on the butt of his pistol.

There was an admixture of admiration and contempt on Maskelyne's face as he said, "Very well, then. Draw him up—but take care!"

When Sean had stepped from the bucket, he stood on the parapet for only a moment before he leaped. He had caught Maskelyne uneasily checking Kate and Beau and knew that his chance was then or never. The last thing Sean remembered was the sound of Kate's scream, clutching the pistol in Maskelyne's left hand as the pan flashed and there was an angry tug at his shirt, and he fell into the darkness. The last thing he remembered thinking was that he had fallen back into the well.

Kate flung herself at Maskelyne, attempting to grab his remaining pistol, but he deftly moved aside and brought the butt of his pistol down on the side of her head. Kate stumbled forward over the low parapet and had she not grasped the chain which held the bucket, she would have plunged headlong into the well.

As Kate wildly tried to regain her balance, she saw that Maskelyne had his weapon up and levelled full at Beau. "Surrender," he cried, "or I'll shoot you as dead as your friend, and the fifty pounds on your head is mine—" then never giving time for an answer, he fired.

Beau stood on the other side of the well, and it seemed that Maskelyne could not miss him at such a distance, but as Kate's eyes blinked at the flash, she felt the bullet strike the iron chin to which she was holding and saw that Beau was safe. Maskelyne saw it too, and flinging away his pistol, he sprang around the well and was at Beau's throat before he knew whether he was hit or not.

Maskelyne was a tall, strong man and about ten years younger than Beau. He thought he would easily have Beau broken down and handcuffed, and then turn to Kate. But he reckoned too carelessly, for though Beau was an inch shorter and older, he was extremely strong and as seasoned as a salted thong. Then they grappled one another and began the terrible struggle, for Beau knew that he was wrestling for his life. And from the look on Maskelyne's face after their first encounter, Kate guessed that Maskelyne knew that the stakes were much the same for him.

As soon as she saw what was happening, Kate warily eased her way back to firm footing, being eager to help Beau. But before she could make a move, she saw that little help of hers was needed, for the Revenue man was flagging. There was a look of anguish and desperate surprise on his face, to find that the man he had thought to master so easily was strong as a giant. They were swaying to and fro, and the Protective man's grip was slackening. His muscles seemed strained and tiring, but Beau held him as firm as a vice. Kate saw from his eyes and the bearing of his body that Beau was gathering himself to give his enemy a fall.

Perhaps Beau would never have had the strength to throw Maskelyne had the captain at that moment not taken one hand off the waist and tried to clutch Beau by the throat. But the only way to avoid most falls is to keep both hands firm between hip and shoulder-blade. The moment Beau felt one hand off his back, he had Maskelyne off his feet and threw him backwards.

Kate did not know whether Beau had been so worn by his fierce struggle that he could not put his fullest strength into the throw, or whether the other, being a very strong and heavy man, needed more to fling him. But instead of Maskelyne going straight down with the back of his head on the floor, as he should have, he staggered backwards a step or two, trying to regain his footing before he went over.

It was those few staggering paces that ruined him, for with the last one he stumbled over the stones close to the mouth of the well. They had been made wet and slippery by the spilt water. Then his heels flew up and he fell backwards with all his weight.

It was then that Kate ran to her brother's fallen body and withdrew the dirk from his belt. At that moment, Beau sprang forward and tried to push Maskelyne into the well, but the younger man grabbed his arm and held it with both hands and so managed to pull himself back onto balance. He then whirled about, and getting Beau's arm over his shoulder, Maskelyne threw Beau to the ground. Before he was able to make a move to follow up his advantage, Kate sprang.

The sight of her brother and the memories of her family had driven Kate to such a fury that the dirk was embedded in Maskelyne's back up to the hilt, a feat which would have been normally beyond even a man's strength. Entering, the dirk sounded as though a melon had been split. Maskelyne gave a bitter cry and there was a wrench on his face when he knew what had happened.

The parapet wall was very low and caught Maskelyne behind the knee as he staggered, tripping him over into the well.

Kate got to the parapet just as Maskelyne fell head first into that black abyss. There was a second of silence, then a dreadful noise like a coconut being broken on a rock, then a deep echoing blow, where he rebounded and struck the wall again, and last of all, the thud and thundering splash, when he reached the water at the bottom. Kate held her breath and listened to see if he would cry out. Yet she knew in her heart that he would never speak again, after that first sickening smash. There was no sound or voice except the moaning voices of the water eddies that she had heard before.

Beau slung himself into the bucket. "See about Sean, but first handle the break," he said to Kate. "Let me down quick into the well." Kate took the break lever, lowering him as quickly as she dared, until she heard the bucket touch water at the bottom, and then went to where Sean had fallen. He was still breathing, but his breath was coming in deep, scraggly rattles. She tore open his shirt and looked at the wound. The bullet seemed to have struck him full in the chest, but at such an angle that it had broken two of his ribs and glanced off without penetrating his body. Kate propped him up against the side of the parapet where, although unconscious, he could breath more comfortably.

Kate sat on the edge of the parapet and listened. All was still, and yet she started once, and could not help looking around over her shoulder, for she still felt as if she were not alone in the well-house. Though she could see no one, still she had the fancy that the spirit of Sir Rodger was hovering about. She guessed now that Captain Maskelyne was not the first man that these walls had seen go headlong down the well.

Beau had been in the well for so long that Kate began to fear that something had happened to him, when he shouted to her to bring him up. So she set the clutch and began pulling the bucket up. From time to time, Kate would stop to look over the parapet, waiting with cramped suspense to see whether Beau would be alone or have something with him. But when the bucket came into sight there was only Beau in it, so she knew that Maskelyne had never come to the top of the water again, and indeed there was little chance he would after that first richochet off the wall of the well. Beau said nothing to Kate, until she spoke:

"Let us fling this jewel down the well after him, Beau. We have come by it in an evil way and it will bring nothing but a curse with it."

At first Beau surprised. Was this the Kate Penhallow who counted her every penny and who had slowly gathered her fortune over years of contraband? Then he remembered the curious religious, even superstitious, streak in Kate.

Kate hesitated for a moment while she half-hoped and yet half-feared he was going to do as she asked; but then he said:

"No, no! But you are overwrought to keep something so precious. Give it to me. It is your treasure and I will never touch a penny of it, except that you give me your leave to—but fling it down the well you will not do. One man has lost his life for it and we have risked ours for it—and may yet lose them for it, too, perhaps."

So Kate gave him the diamond.

Chapter 21

While Beau and Sean were negotiating with the Amsterdam diamond merchants, Messrs. Brand and Roosfeld, and Lydia was caring for the inn, Kate was in Bristol preparing passage for Beau and herself to the New World.

"To hell with Bristol and its damned dismal weather," she muttered between clenched teeth. She had always deemed Bristol the dreariest of seaports, even when the weather was good, which was not often.

"You desire Mr. Norton, Ma'am?" Norton and Mason's senior clerk fluttered visibly. Seldom did so gracious a vision as Kate Penhallow brighten the firm's offices.

"Please inform him that Miss Penhallow is here,"

she said, tightening a scarf which secured a new white beaver hat.

The man bowed stiffly from the waist, his arms held rigidly at his sides. "Yes, m'lady. He shall be informed directly of your arrival."

A coal fire crackled invitingly in the grate of the long, desk-barricaded room; to it she held out a slim foot protected against the muddy slush of the streets by a dainty boot of gray leather trimmed with squirrel.

Though pleased by the admiring stares from several pale-faced clerks, she was nonetheless irritated by the monotonous scratch-scratching of their pens. Kate continued an aimless circuit of the accounting room.

How was she looking? Confoundedly like the witch of Endor, no doubt. She peered warily into a small mirror, the silvering of which had begun to peel away. There looked out at her an undeniably attractive face, but from beneath the beaver hat, a single curl peeked out. Irritated, she noted that it revealed traces of powder. She wet her fingers and pushed the curl back under the brim.

Attracted by a dull thundering which made the floor quiver, she strolled over to a window and lingered there. A line of carts was entering a passage situated directly below the office. It permitted freight to be hauled into a courtyard and in turn made it possible for cargo to roll up alongside of ships lying to either side of Norton and Mason's T-shaped wharf. By raising her eyes, Kate could make out dozens of similar warehouses, mostly unpainted and dingy. Beyond them rose a confused tangle of spars and rigging. In the smoke-dimmed sky a few untidy-looking gulls flapped aimlessly.

Bemoaning the sleep she had lost on the journey to Bristol, Kate drew a deep breath and became intrigued with the idea of identifying as many as she could of such a multitude of odors. Nostrils crinkled, she listed: fish, tar, tobacco, turpentine, paint, and a strangely erotic odor of cured hides. Most provocative of all was a blend of spices: cloves, cinnamon, ginger and pepper.

Restless, she crossed to the street side of the office and stood looking out on a depressing vista of tiles, shingles and sullenly smoking chimneys. There were dozens, hundreds of chimneys, each spewing out a tendril of sulphurous black smoke which, climbing a few yards, dropped soot on the pools of rain on the roofs.

Below, a dray was clattering over greasy-looking cobbles. The big horses pulling it leaned into their collars and set down their shaggy feet as if weary to death. The driver sat hunched over with a battered three-cornered hat pulled low over his face. In the dray was a huge coil of hawser, a maul and a couple of barrels. On its tail board two small ragged boys perched like grimy sparrows. To either side of the street below, old, old houses leaned toward each other like a weary team of plough horses. The passing dray forced a woman with a market basket to flatten against a wall already stained by flying mub. Her shrill curses rose, but the driver never lifted his head.

"There can't be an uglier city in the whole world," Kate decided, turning away from the dirty panes.

She preferred the windows looking out on the ships and the harbour. Her interest stirred. One of Norton and Mason's vessels was casting off. Out on the wharf she recognized Mr. Norton's plump, short-legged figure. The considerable bustle and hilarity which usually attended a ship's departure was strangely lacking. Today, the knot of men remaining on the wharf stood close together, silently watching her high sides begin to slide slowly away.

"My good man," Kate said. "Where is that ship for. India? Italy?"

Mr. Motley, the chief clerk, nearly upset the ink in his eagerness to be of service. "No, m'lady. The *Western Flyer* is bound for New York."

"New York?" Kate gave the weary old man a dazzling smile.

"Yes, m'lady. New York is one of the major ports in the New World."

Poor little man, could he ever be bold? He looked so thin, and his eyes were red, too—but not from hearty red wines.

North America? Suddenly, the New World seemed a very strange and forbidding place. In all her years, Kate could not recall meeting any Americans other than Beau. She must have met many of them of course, but only the gentleman from New Orleans had made any lasting impression. And he had floated into her life, literally, from the sea. Why had he made such a definite impression? Perhaps even because in the early mornings hours in the inn, when candles were guttering and the air grew stale about the gaming table, there had been a vitality, a breath of freshness about him suggestive of sunny woods and windy fields. As she stood there, peering blankly out on the harbour's gray water, she especially recalled the way he sat a horse as he rode over the moors. She fancied she would always remember the ineffable grace with which he would clear a three-bar gate, despite his inevitable hangover. It had been remarkable how they had taken to one another. Poor Beau! How badly he had bungled his chances to make a good and decent life for himself! It would all be different now!

"It's just as well we met when we did," she thought "If he were a younger man, Beau I would never have gotten along. Too damned much alike." Still she wondered.

"Does the tobacco I am smelling come from Virginia?" Kate asked suddenly.

Mr. Motley said, "Yes, m'lady, almost all of the firm's tobacco is grown in Virginia."

She turned so that she might have a better view of the wooden hogsheads barely visible through the door of a warehouse. Beau had once said that a cousin of his grew tobacco in Virginia. Kate was amused to think that some of the brown leaves stored below might have sprouted on the land of Beau's cousin!

Mr. Motley bustled on, chafing chilled hands and pretending to be busy, as Mr. Norton walked into the room. At the sight of Kate standing so tall and composed before the window, Mr. Norton's plump little figure bowed so profoundly that a topknot of gray hair clinging to the glassy surface of his scalp became visible.

"A pleasure, Miss Penhallow, and the richer for

being unanticipated." Suddenly he glared about the counting room. "Why has Miss Penhallow been kept waiting out here? She should have been shown into my private office. Motley, come here!" The old clerk slid down from his stool and, as he hurried forward, thrust his goose quill behind his ear, deepening an inky smudge already marking the pink flesh below his yellowed wig.

"What in blazes d'you mean by keeping Miss Penhallow waiting out here?"

Blinking, Mr. Motley faltered back half a step. "Why, why, Mr. Norton, I didn't think there was a fire going in your office, sir."

"There is always a fire going in my office! Have you no wits? Of course there's a fire." Norton knew perfectly well it was so tiny that it threw little heat.

The old clerk cringed in such abject fear that Kate felt sickened.

"Confound it, Motley, I fear you have not sense enough to be a chief clerk!" growled Norton, blowing his nose. "On Friday, you'll go back to being a simple senior clerk—very simple!"

Motley's dull face twitched. In appeal he held out a hand covered with swollen blue veins. "Oh, oh, no! Please, sir, I beg you! I couldn't stand the disgrace. All my life I have worked for this. I do my best to give satisfaction, sir."

Kate observed the avid gaze of the other clerks. They looked too brutally hopeful.

"Please, as a favor to me, let Motley keep on as chief clerk," she begged. "I really preferred being out here."

"You did?"

She trained her most devasting smile on him. "Yes, in truth. You know, Mr. Norton, how I hate being alone. It gives me the megrims. From in here I could see the ships."

She never forgot the old clerk's look of passionate gratitude when Mr. Norton, again loudly blowing his nose, grunted: "Since Miss Penhallow intercedes—but mind your step, do you hear? Now then, Motley, you—and the rest of you stop your stupid gawking. D'you think I pay you ten and six to sit gaping like yokels at a fair? Be at your work, or you'll be on the street come Friday!"

To Kate it was utterly astounding that anybody so small and insignificant as Mr. Norton culd inspire such abject terror. All for ten and six, too. Merciful heavens! It dawned on her that these poor creatures must *live* on such a sum! No, they didn't live; they merely existed, like old shoes that had not yet been thrown out.

Flushed, she followed the merchant into a small office littered with a multitude of dusty ships' models, renderings of new vessels and queer samples of merchandise. The room smelt of mice. And sure enough, she spied two holes. One was in the far corner of the mop boarding, the other behind the leg of Norton's desk. Private signal flags framed behind glass hung on the walls. A sketch on the desk intrigued her enough to pick it up.

"What a lovely ship!"

"She's a brig, Ma'am. Ships have three masts."

"Well, despite your distinctions, sir, she's beautiful. Exquisite! There is poetry to her lines. *Yankee Clipper*? What an odd name. Is she yours?"

Norton smiled, shook his head. "No, she's building in New York. My partner saw her, fancied her lines and bribed one of the shipwrights to copy her dimensions." He pursed his lips. "She's too pretty to be profitable, I fear. But if the *Yankee Clipper* proves fast, why—we'll build us one like her. Maybe two."

"But is that—well, is that done?"

Mr. Norton's smile was tolerant. "Of course. Mason writes she is being built by a rival. He'd copy a vessel of ours quite as quickly. Pray seat yourself."

Norton helped her to an armchair smelling of mildew and dust. It faced a tiny open fire. After removing a sherry-colored surtout and hanging his beaver hat to a hook, the merchant placed a small lump of coal on the grate.

"Better, eh?" he suggested and, turning his back to the hearth, warmed his palms behind plump buttocks.

"It *is* cold here. I vow I can see my breath."

"Heat dulls the wits I find, Miss Penhallow. These sudden cold and rainy days I find delightful," he observed, looking down at the charming young woman frankly sprawled in the chair. Damned handsome legs on her, long and neat and with slender ankles. Suddenly he felt his years.

"Cards again, or was it the races?" He scowled slyly at her. "Or is it your shipping business?"

"Prodigious bad luck with everything. Alas! No horse seems to go as fast as the money I wager on him. I seem to give all my best cards to my friends," she replied, looking not at him but into the coals. "And I have recently gone out of the shipping business."

"I regret to hear it."

"Thank you, Mr. Norton. Fact is, I stand in temporary need of money. And passage to the New World."

Methodically, Mr. Norton produced a snuff box of tortoise shell from his coat tail, helped himself to a pinch.

"May I remind you, Ma'am, that there is a war on, and that Norton and Mason are already at some loss for ships?" He cocked his head at the ceiling. "It could not be much worse, nor our prices more outrageous."

"Yes, I know it all too well." Kate smiled wryly and one of her legs began to nervously swing, the one that Mr. Norton had been admiring in particular. "I—I well, I must borrow against my word."

Norton permitted himself the most delicate of shrugs, studied the lid of his snuff box. "That would be most difficult, Ma'am. Instead, why not sell some of your holdings in Cornwall. Let us say the inn?"

Kate laughed and spread her hands. "That, my dear Mr. Norton—well, no."

"Well, then, the other investments that your father left you?"

Kate raised a palm before her lips and blew away some invisible object.

Norton's brows merged. "The moor land then? Surely that's not gone?"

"Oh, no. Papa entailed it. But I have rented it for twenty years."

"How much a year?"

"A mere five hundred guineas, but—"

Mr. Norton's disapproval was mixed with relief. "You've been had! It's worth a thousand at the least. Still, with five hundred you can manage."

A grimace troubled Kate's bright face. "The rent has been paid for twenty years in advance. That is why I was prepared to sell the inn so cheaply to that lady from London—oh, what was her name? Lydia something."

Mr. Norton looked genuinely alarmed. "My dear child, don't tell me you've lost that value as well?"

Gossamer scarf ends fluttered faintly to Kate's nod. "Every farthing of it. I have made nothing but the most monstrous mistakes in these last months. Plague take me!"

"But all that silverware? The tapestries?"

"The shylocks have them, Mr. Norton. My luck has been infernally bad this year."

"God's my life! I can believe it." The little merchant groaned and mopped his head which had suddenly become wet. When he sneezed over his snuff he couldn't take the least pleasure in it. To think of losing that much money. Why, most merchants would give a year's profit for what this woman had lost in a few months!

"What of the jewels? Surely—"

Kate raised that subborn curl from her ear. Her slender fingers, Norton noticed, were stripped of rings.

"I vow, Mr. Norton, you are slow to understand. All I have left is this one smart gown and a chest of garments too out of mode for the high-priced shylocks to consider."

"But your friends? You've dozens of them."

Norton's fat little face was puckered into worried amazement that made Kate almost laugh. "But I knew your father, Kate; he was a man of some nobility and profit. Surely—"

"'Tea and trade nobility,'" Kate corrected. She bent forward, extending slender hands to the kindling blaze. "Yes, Mr. Norton, you'd have no task finding plenty of homely cats whose families fought for the Magna Carta, vastly hopeful of beholding—" she raised a whimsical eyebrow— "those shapely limbs garbed in sackcloth and ashes, and the less sackcloth the better."

Kate Penhallow arose with graceful deliberation and moved over to the window. It had begun to rain, she noticed, and here she was without the price of a chair.

"Now do you see, Mr. Norton, why I shall be hard pressed to go to the New World?"

"All too well," came the deliberate reply.

Norton went over to his desk and picked up a newspaper. He sat down and thumbed through it until he found an article. He didn't like what he had to say. There was something about old Penhallow's frantically impractical daughter which fascinated, even while it horrified him.

"Have you read the news today?"

"I fear I read very little."

"Well, you had better read this."

"No. You read it—give me the tone of it."

"Very well," the little man somberly agreed, replacing the single folded-over sheet. "In brief, there is a war on with France, Miss Penhallow. And the French have tightened their embargo against

240

English shipping. I don't think we will be sending more ships to the Colonies. We have lost to many already."

"Why do you keep calling the Colonies the Colonies, Mister Norton? I thought they had gained their independence."

Mr. Norton rustled himself uneasily. "An old habit, Miss Penhallow. The point is, our ships are embargoed. The Colonies are sympathic to the French."

"Embargoed?" Kate murmured. "What a fascinating word! Beau and Sean would love it. What does it mean?"

"It means, Miss Penhallow, that the Colonies—er, the Americas—are not available for our goods."

"But why? What has the firm done?"

"I don't mean just this firm's goods, Ma'am. The embargo applies to all British shipping."

"How strange that war should interfere with commerce. Of prodigious interest, no doubt, but what can this have to do with my unhappy affairs?"

"I fear, Miss Penhallow, it will add to your long tally of woes."

"What do you mean?" She faced him, maintaining her incredulity, for she knew that all depended upon her demeanor. She clamped down hard on the back of a chair. "Are you trying to say that you are unable to provide me with passage to the New World?"

His homely round face filled with concern, Norton got up from his desk and came forward. "It isn't that I will not provide you with passage, Miss Penhallow, but that I can not. You and, if I may say so, others more urgently in need of passage are not likely to receive while this war lasts. And you can make your mind up to that."

Like blows of a wooden club striking a block, the words thudded in Kate's ears. A curious breathlessness gripped her. Wide-eyed, she tried to concentrate on what the plump little man before her was saying.

"Mark my words, Ma'am, before a year is out there'll be many a trading house struggling for it's life, many a firm with it's doors closed forever. You will see those wharfs out there choked with idle ships. It will probably not interest you, but back in '69 and '70, your father and we learned what an embargo can do. This time I intend to be better prepared."

"Then you can secure me no passage to the Americas?"

"I might wish to aid you, Miss Penahllow. Your father was a stout friend in the old days, when our firm was first beginning—bought shares when we needed a new ship." Mr. Norton shifted uneasily. He did not like to discuss the founding of his company. "It was a sound investment, of course; still it helped us," he concluded lamely.

"Then I should do no less than my father did," Kate said brightly. "Since you will send no ships to the Americas for as long as the war lasts, God spare us, and since you will have so many standing idle, perhaps I could arrange the purchase of a ship?"

"A ship, you say? And where would you be finding the money for that, you who were destitute a moment ago?"

"I still have the inn," Kate said demurely. "Perhaps I could arrange to raise ten thousand pounds on that, in addition to what I have already been paid. Of course, the money is not due yet, but I think perhaps—"

A sly look came into Mr. Norton's eyes. "Ah, so you do have some monies available then?" He sat back down behind his desk. "Let us say fifteen thousand pounds."

"Twelve thousand—and I'm not sure how I will raise the extra two," Kate said worriedly.

"Very well, then, twelve," said Mr. Norton, vastly relieved.

"And let it be the *Yankee Clipper*. I like the look of her."

"You have your father's eye for a ship. Very well, then, let it be the *Yankee Clipper*."

Twelve thousand pounds, Mr. Norton thought when Kate had left; how fortunate to have rid himself of one more ship. As he lit his pipe, a worried look crossed his forehead. Had he been taken advantage of again. Once could never tell with the Penhallows.

As Kate stepped into the rainy street, she smiled. She had come to Bristol prepared to pay any price for even a berth aboard a ship. Now she had acquired an entire ship, and for only twelve thousand pounds! Of course, there would be the costs of the crew and some repairs, there were always repairs, but how easily she had let the old man fall into his own trap. As if you could take advantage of a Penhallow!

Chapter 22

When the transactions had been completed with the
Amsterdam diamond merchants, Messrs. Brand and
Roosfeld, Kate and Beau and Sean found themselves wealthy beyond their wildest expectations, a
wealth made even greater, in Sean's case by the
considerable dowry which Lydia brought him.

Having learned a bitter lesson in the past, when
their pardon was upheld by the courts, in gratitude
Beau and Sean laid out a portion of their newly
found fortune in good works. With Kate, they
rebuilt and enlarged the almshouses beyond all that
Sir Rodger Mohune could have ever thought of, and
so established them to be a haven for all worn-out
sailors of that coast. Next, they sought the guidance
of Reverend Castallack and the Brethren of the

Trinity and built a lighthouse on the headland to be a Channel beacon for sea-going ships, so that they might not be led ashore by wreckers in the future. Lastly, they beautified the church, throwing out the cumbrous oak seats and neatly pewing it with leather covered ones. Much of the old glass they also caused to be removed, and reglazed all the windows tight against the wind. With a new high pulpit, reading-desk, and altar, there was not a church in the countryside which could vie with that of their village. The great vault below the church, with its memories, was set in order and then sealed up, so that nothing was ever heard of the Mohune legends again.

The village, too, renewed itself with the new almshouses and church. There were old houses rebuilt and fresh ones reared and set out for hire. Carnforth Inn was refurbished by Sean and Lydia and again made open to the public, so that people from as far away as Camelford came to stay there, and any shipwrecked or travel-worn sailor found board and welcome within its doors.

Curiously, it was not Kate but Sean who bought the great Manor House, and Lydia who once more turned it into a stately home, with trim lawns and terraced balustrades, where they could sit and see the thin blue smoke hang above the village on summer evenings. Sean and Lydia rarely left their village, being well content to see the dawn tipping the long line of cliffs with gold and the night walking in dew across the meadows; to watch the spring clothe the beech boughs with green or the figs ripen on the southern wall, while behind all is spread, as a curtain, the eternal sea, ever the same and ever changing. Yet Sean loved the sea best when it was lashed to a madness in the autumn gale, and to hear the grinding roar and churn of pebbles like a great organ playing all night. It was then he would turn in bed and thank God, more from the heart, perhaps, than any other living man, that he was not fighting for his life on Moontide Beach.

Over three thousand miles away, Kate Penhallow's pen whispered across the ledger before her. Her accounts for the brigantine *Gilded Lady II* showed that, what with wharfage, pilotage, and the food for the voyage to Boston, Harbor Expenses had risen from $47.86 to $50.22. At this rate, Penhallow and d'Auberge Shipping Ltd. would have to raise their prices—or absorb the costs into their profits. It was enough to made Kate Penhallow weep.

Instead, she paused, yawned, and picking up a horn- handled penknife resharpened her goose quill. Dust drifting about the drafty, rat-infested warehouse filled her eyes, make them heavy. A sad monotonous chant raised by stevedores hoisting the brigantine's cargo inboard was beginning to grate on her nerves. Since six she had been driving this pen over what seemed like an endless succession of ledgers, invoices, manifests and bills of lading. Her fingers felt so stiff and wooden they might have belonged to someone else.

From time to time she turned to peer out a window at her back. It was so veiled by cobwebs she could barely make out *Gilded Lady II's* weathered grayed spars against a cold blue sky. Sweating in the cold winter sunshine, Beau heaved harder than any of the sniffling stevedores. He drove them hard, though, because he knew under this stiff west wind the tide would ebb early and he was, as always, impatient, not to lose a moment. Kate rested a little, watching the gray gulls wheel and mew above the brigantine's tops. Now and then they swooped very low. They were hopeful of a smashed cask or barrel.

The pimpled, half-grown youth Beau dignified with the title of shipping clerk turned a stupid, freckled face. "Was it one or two kegs o' molasses for Weldon & Co., Ma'am?"

"Three. For pity's sake, three! And mind you, don't let those careless bastards drive a bale hook into the flour sacks. They go as a part of Monk's and Peabody's order."

A spring bell tinkled hysterically; then a swarthy man with an enormous wart on the side of his chin clumped in from the street. A quid of tobacco bulged like the mumps in one of his grimy cheeks.

"Howdy. Heerd tell you is lookin' for deck hands."

"That's so," Kate admitted briskly. "And you can take off your hat in my presence."

The intruder stared for a moment, but complied. He seemed highly amused. "Wal, I got a pair o' niggers outside—likely sailors. Seein it's you, Ma'am, I reckon you can sign 'em on for a dollar and a half a day—apiece—and found."

A dollar and fifty cents! Kate's tall figure stiffened on the stool to counteract the sinking in her heart. Right now Penhallow and d'Auberge needed additional hands, but their cash balance was low.

The building of a second and third brigantine was costing more than they had expected. Too much was already invested in the old brigantine lying out there with the flood tide making up under her heel. Still, one could not let any human being remain in slavery when there was honest work to be had. Kate thought hard. She had been hoping to pick up a couple of hands for the next voyage at seventy-five cents apiece. That was five cents below the lowest current wage. In New York, it was reckoned a five-day trip to Boston in the wintertime. But the *Gilded Lady II* was so old and slow she couldn't count on reaching Boston in under seven days. Twice seven was fourteen, then there would be a week in port up there. Numbly her fingers flew over a mental slate. Sixty-three dollars! That left Beau and herself not a dime to go and come on without touching capital. It was clear she couldn't afford to pay even seventy-five cents. At sixty-five, the bill would be forty-five and a half Spanish dollars.

Said Kate, pushing the dusty hair from her eyes, "A dollar and a half! Mister, I never heard of such nonsense—not even from a slave dealer!"

The intruder sniffed, shifted his chew and rolled a bleary eye. "Seein's it's you, Ma'am, I'll let you sign them niggers for a dollar a day an' found."

Kate gave him a sweet smile. "I will sign them on at sixty cents."

The slave owner's unshaved jaw sagged. "What's that?"

"You heard me. That's a good price," Kate informed him staunchly. "Aren't many ships clearing this time of the year, and you know it!"

"Where's yer vessel for?"

"Boston. She will be back here inside of a month. You might just as well get those hands of yours out of your barracoon and earning money instead of eating their heads off."

Grubbing in his nose with a dirty forefinger, the slave dealer deliberated. "Eighty-five cents a day," he grunted. "And you can take it or leave it."

"Sixty," said Kate again, slipping off her stool. She dusted hands seasoned by the winds and work, and pointedly ignoring the slave dealer, went over to check some invoices. It was easy to act mean; she was feeling uncommonly spiteful. Not twenty minutes before two women from her church circle strolled by all decked out in white beaver hats tied with silk string under their chins. They were the rage and they knew she knew it, even if she didn't own one. She could have killed them both for their smug look of commiseration when they noticed her bent over a ledger with her skirt tucked up and the stripes of her old outer petticoat in plain sight. They had not come in they had just minced along giggling, with their silly heads together. *That's all right,* Kate thought, *I can buy and sell you—and your fathers!*

From the tail of her eye she noticed Beau quit work directing the storage to talk with a Mr. Alston. She recognized him as a tidesman from the Customs House. *I wonder what that's all about,* she thought. *I'll hear about it this evening at supper.*

Kate jumped at the slave dealer's sudden, "You win." Having surveyed the gleanings from his nose, he jerked a curt nod. "Take 'em then for sixty-five."

If he expected appreciation on Kate's part, he was

disappointed.

"I warrant you take advantage of my sex, sir," Kate demurred. "Let me see these sailors."

The dealer thrust his battered head out of the door. "You Hosiah, Benjamin, come heah!"

An undersized black, so round-shouldered as to look hunchbacked, shambled in after wiping caked mud from his naked feet. The office then darkened momentarily at the entrance of a huge slave. His skin gave off a grayish-blue tone rather than chocolate-brown, and there were some tribal scars on his cheeks. They were arranged in a crude chevron pattern. His front teeth had been filed into blunt points. He moved slowly because a stout chain joined two rings welded about his ankles. Both the blacks clawed off red woolen stocking caps, then stood staring at the gritty planking beneath their feet.

"You can send that last man out," Kate ordered sharply. "Mr. d'Auberge doesn't want any trouble-makers aboard."

"Benjamin ain't no trouble-maker, Ma'am, onct he'd aboard ship. He's a fine deck hand."

"Nonsense! He's a blue nigger; you can't fool me. Once a mean nigger always a mean nigger." Kate pointed to a tip of a welt showing about the neckband of the big black's ragged shirt. "The deception of you offering me a nigger with whip marks still hot on his back! And this other one! Why, he's not strong enough to pull a spoon from a pot!" Her last objection was entirely perfunctory, and Kate knew it; there were big muscles in the shorter seaman's legs and arms.

Hesitantly, the giant slave's tawny eyes climbed and fixed themselves on Kate. He did it in a hopeless, miserable sort of way. She could tell he knew he was not going to be signed on and, because of that, he would get another taste of the slave dealer's rawhide whip.

He was wrong. Five minutes later Hosiah and Benjamin were contracted for as ordinary seamen at sixty-five cents a day—and found.

"Now here's the way it will be," Kate said firmly. "You will work one voyage. If you prove able seamen, I'll buy you." Kate looked them over carefully. "I should be able to get you for about a hundred dollars apiece. Then you'll ship with Penhallow and d'Auberge until you have paid back that money and another one hundred dollars apiece for my investment. After that you'll be free men, to continue working for us or seek work elsewhere. Do you understand?"

The two blacks nodded vigorously and began speaking happily to each other in some language Kate had never heard before.

"If you prove unsatisfactory, you'll work your time out, with my profit," Kate continued, "then you'll be set loose to find employment elsewhere. In a word, you'll be let go. Do you understand?"

The tall black man looked down at the smaller man as if for help, but Hosiah was looking at him with equal puzzlement. Kate saw her mistake at once. It was no good trying to explain to a slave what it meant to be without work. Kate sat back down on the stool. "Now, Hosiah, you get out to the wharf and set to work," she flung at the hunchback. "Tell

Mr. d'Auberge I hired you."

"Yassum, and de Lawd bless you. Hit's a powerful slim rations in dat ol' barracoon."

The tall blue-black's hands made ineffectual little motions. He was trying to say something but couldn't.

"Be quiet with your nonsense, Ben." Kate understood blacks better than most. Blue niggers, she knew, were prouder than the brown ones. Whipping seldom made any impression on them. She picked up the key the slave dealer had left on the desk and tossed it to Ben. "You can unfasten that padlock. I reckon you have better sense than to try to run away."

"Oh! Yassum! Yassum. Ben work bestis he kin."

He bent. His thick fingers quivered so hard he could not turn the key right away. Still kneeling, he looked up and his twany eyes gave her a look, immeasureably pitiful, yet somehow dignified.

"Give me that lock! You'd likely spoil it!" Kate's tone was sharp. She felt ready to burst into tears. "Now, you just get out of here and go to work."

"Yessum."

Fetter ends clanking, the giant man backed out past a heap of bear and 'coonskin Kate had wheedled away from a lone hunter fresh in from the mountains of Pennsylvania.

Mercurially, her mood changed and, humming, she climbed back firmly on the high stool. For those skins she had paid next to nothing. And to think of having signed on two strong hands at sixty-five cents a day! The savings would buy quite a lot of victuals! What with ducks and seafood so abundant, she and

252

Beau ought to make out all right for the next five weeks. Why, they would not need to touch capital at all!

Kate was sanding the Monks and Peabody invoice when Beau came in, perspiration gleaming on his cheeks, emphasizing some nearly invisible lines that were developing. More sweat ran in rivulets down to the base of his neck and stained his shirt. Kate smiled at a small smear of tar on his forehead.

"My God! Haven't you finished?"

"Yes, Beau, just this minute. It took time to reckon Hancock's order." Kate hesitated. "The Coastwise tax on tobacco is a shilling a hundred weight, isn't it?"

"Told you so fifty times. Where's Houghton and Sons' manifest? Where is it? Come on, find it! The pilot is here."

In silence Kate flipped through the manifests.

Beau pointed to the furs. "How did that trash get in here?"

"A trapper came in from around Pittsburgh. He needed money and I got them very cheap. I thought I'd send them along on this voyage as part of my share."

"Don't be a fool. They have more bears in Massachusetts than they have in Pennsylvania."

He was mad.

"Maybe, honey, but not so good as these," Kate placated with a smile. "See how beautifully they're tanned. The fur won't come out. Pull it and see. I got all five for less than twenty dollars and six 'coons thrown in. It was too good to miss."

She was right and Beau knew it, and that made him madder. What with doing three men's work, he was worn out, and he'd jammed a splinter under his thumbnail.

"Where'd you find those last two hands?"

Raising a beamy if dusty countenance, Kate told him. But Beau was pulling on his coat, not looking in her direction.

"You didn't hire much," said Beau, digging at the splinter with his penknife. "One is humpbacked and the other is mean. Why couldn't you find me a couple of decent men?"

Kate stared at him, round-eyed. "Why I had to take what we could afford. Why, Beau, why don't you ask how much I paid for them?"

"Well?"

"I got them for sixty-five cents a day—each."

"Oh, you did, eh? Well, I said they weren't worth much!"

Kate laughed, a wild quivering laugh, her eyes closed. And to think that she had wanted to be the lady of the Manor. This was her world! In another couple of years, she would have three, maybe five ships, and trading as far away as the West Indies. Yes, this was her world.

GARBAGE WORLD
Charles Platt

BT51164 $1.25
Science Fiction

Two completely opposite cultures meet when the super-sanitary inhabitants of the Pleasure Worlds suddenly find they need the help of those who live in Garbage World—its filth encrusted inhabitants. Reissue.

THE SPANISH CHAPEL
Dorothy Daniels

BT51165 $1.25
Gothic

Someone in the Moreno family was doomed to die when the spirit of the dead monk and nun came to pray in the Spanish Chapel. Donna Moreno scoffed at the legend at first ... but the overpowering shadow of the Spanish Chapel and the menacing things that began to happen in the gloomy fortress-like mansion frightened her ... then turned to absolute terror. Reissue.

THE NEVADA GUN
Gordon D. Shirreffs

BT51166 $1.25
Western

One by one they eliminated the occupants of the Lazy Z Ranch until it held only one female. It was almost theirs ... then Vic Standish rode in to give her a hand ... and his gun. Reissue.

LAST MAN ALIVE
Gordon D. Shirreffs

BT51167 $1.25
Western

A lone survivor of a wagon train massacre is pitted against a more treacherous foe than the Indians ... a foe determined not to see him the last man alive. Reissue.

SEND TO: BELMONT TOWER BOOKS
P.O. Box 270
Norwalk, Connecticut 06852

Please send me the following titles:

Quantity	Book Number	Price
_____	_____	_____
_____	_____	_____
_____	_____	_____
_____	_____	_____
_____	_____	_____

In the event we are out of stock on any of your selections, please list alternate titles below.

_____	_____	_____
_____	_____	_____
_____	_____	_____
_____	_____	_____

Postage/Handling _____

I enclose . . . . . . _____

FOR U.S. ORDERS, add 35¢ per book to cover cost of postage and handling. Buy five or more copies and we will pay for shipping. Sorry no C.O.D.'s.

FOR ORDERS SENT OUTSIDE THE U.S.A.
Add $1.00 for the first book and 25¢ for each additional book. PAY BY foreign draft or money order drawn on a U.S. bank, payable in U.S. ($) dollars.
☐ Please send me a free catalog.

NAME_____
(Please print)

ADDRESS_____

CITY _____ STATE _____ ZIP _____
Allow Four Weeks for Delivery